Four Bare Legs in a Bed

Four Bare Legs in a Bed

Helen Simpson

HARMONY BOOKS/NEW YORK

Published by Harmony Books, a division of
Crown Publishers, Inc., 201 East 50th Street,
New York, New York 10022.
Member of the Crown Publishing Group.

Originally published in Great Britain by
William Heinemann Limited in 1990.
HARMONY and colophon are trademarks of
Crown Publishers, Inc.

Manufactured in the United States of America

Library of Congress Cataloging-in-Publication Data

Simpson, Helen.
Four bare legs in a bed / Helen Simpson.
p. cm.
I. Title. II. Title: 4 bare legs in a bed.
PR6069.I4226F68   1992
823'.914—dc20   91-25762
                                                       CIP

ISBN 0-517-58508-1
10 9 8 7 6 5 4 3 2 1
First American Edition

Contents

Four Bare Legs
in a Bed

When you draw the curtains in the morning you stand in front of the window like a black dog. I am brought down to earth with a bump. It isn't fair.

'Where were *you* last night?'

You ask, even though you *know* we were sitting side by side over a shepherd's pie in front of *World in Action*. I sip my tea and blink at the little azure Chinaman fishing from his pagoda.

'*Well?*' you insist.

I channel vertically under the sheet to hide my blushing neck, muttering demulcent nothings. Goats and monkeys.

What can I say, after all? I can hardly admit that I had a most colourful and stimulating night, thank you, lying bear-hugged with your squash partner skin to skin, dissolving in an exchange of slow damp kisses.

Don't let on to the Old Man, but I think I can safely say I have slept with all the men and boys of my acquaintance, including the grey-beards and one-way homosexuals and those towards whom I had not thought I felt an iota of oestrus.

Only two nights ago I was lying on a riverbank with the other girls, and beside me knelt a boy of about fourteen or fifteen, a childish little chap. A boatload of his schoolfriends in their uniforms drifted past. They wore straw hats, but the sun beat up from the river to make crescents of light flick like sticklebacks over their faces. As they floated by, their smarmy teacher unleashed on us a particularly obsequious grin. His teeth were snaggled and tarnished. Ooh, we all giggled, revolted, and my little boy showed himself in sympathy. I gave him a kiss and a hug; there was a beam of envy from the schoolmaster. I gave him more hugs and kisses, and a generous warmth spread through me, tantalising and lovely.

'You're only fourteen, aren't you, darling,' I teased, pressing his head to my bosom, pretending to be motherly. I woke describing circles, and I was laughing.

When we were first married, all of six months ago, he used to bring home large men in suits who laughed loudly, drank beer from tins and said outlandish things in suddenly solemn voices: for example, 'It's time to put your cock on the block,' and, 'We are talking serious megabucks.' After a couple of months he stopped inviting them. I missed the flick of their eyes, but by then of course we were talking serious monogamy.

A couple of nights before the wedding we met for a drink on Eel Pie Island. We stood in the long grass staring upstream, watching the Thames flow by on either side, dividing just before it reached us and meeting again behind us. I looked back down half-a-dozen years and saw my

2

secret self at thirteen or fourteen. I had never felt incomplete alone, nor had I ever trembled for security. Now I had a premonition that my privacy and self-possession, which harmed nobody and were my only important treasures, would be things of the past the day after tomorrow. My saying yes to a wedding appeared in this illuminated instant as self-betrayal. A tide of shame and terror crept over my skin, moving fast like spilt wine. I stammered some thin wedge of these thoughts to my future husband, thinking (with an early marital shudder at the predictability), he will say no man is an island.

'No man is an island,' he said.

Incidentally, marriage gave his words the lie, since it made an island of every man except himself. Conjugal life correctly conjugated reads: libido libidas libidat libidamus libidatis libiDON'T. Goodbye to the pure uncomplicated glee which can spring up between strangers, leading them out of their clothes and towards each other in a spirit of, among other things, sunny friendship.

The girls at school had a quasi-religious conviction that once you felt the right way about a man, that was *it*. He was the other half who would make you whole, he was the only possible father of your children. I meet Rhoda every once in a while for a slice of cauliflower quiche, and she still subscribes to all that.

'Either it's Animal Lust, which doesn't last,' says Rhoda, 'or it's the Real Thing, which means Marriage.' Rhoda likes things cut and dried. Recently she became engaged to the only possible father of her children. She took him shopping for a ring, hauled him past the windows of Hatton Garden, and he expressed nothing but ridicule at the prices. Next time he went to tea with

3

Rhoda's parents, he was sitting on the edge of the sofa balancing a plate of flapjacks on his knee when his prospective mother-in-law produced a tray of unpriced rings and demanded that he choose one. She said her daughter Rhoda was not to be shamed by a naked finger. He chose, and of course it turned out to be the second most expensive, over a thousand. There is a moral in that somewhere.

Sometimes I slide my ring off before we go to a party, but he makes me put it on again. That left-handed ring finger is the weakest of the ten, always the first to let you down during a vigorous scherzando; there are sets of arpeggios based exclusively round strengthening its feebleness. It is also the most sensitive, the one women use when following such instructions as, Pat this feather-weight creme lightly into the fragile skin tissue which surrounds the eye area.

Lily-livered, swathed in white from head to foot, I said, 'I will.' Willing and waking may come to the same thing, but sleep is another matter. I am only properly alone now when I'm asleep, such is the encroachment. Well, sleep is a third part of life so I suppose I mustn't grumble.

You don't even have a right to your own bed when you're married. There is no escaping the mildmint breath toothpasting its way across the pillows. I am lying cool and straight in my bed when *he* climbs in with a proprietorial air, and I catch myself thinking, 'How dare you.' I never achieve the old full secrecy now, I never properly escape him, not until I've lost consciousness altogether. And even then ... The other night as I lay waiting for sleep – almost there – I felt his fingertips on my eyelids, and I knew he was testing whether the eyeballs were moving in order to tell whether I was dreaming or not.

My husband is older than me; not so much older that he thanks his lucky stars for me, but sufficiently older to create the distance of a demi-generation gap between us. He is a Management Consultant and he thinks he's got me taped. He probably has, except for my nocturnal life. He has a square leonine head with icy blue-green eyes. I don't know what he thinks about – 'If only he could talk,' as old people say of their pets.

You could say we rushed into it, but then, why *not* repent at leisure. How dismal are those long-term liaisons where, the seven years and a day being up, no nerve is left to take the plunge. On our honeymoon near St Ives, there was one late wordless picnic down on the beach when I stared at his cleanly minted profile against the night sky and worshipped the silence. Out last week at some busy new restaurant, however, we sat dumbly over plates of chilli-spiced pomfret fish until in the end, to stop the water-drops leaping, I lowered my eyes, staring hard at his tee-shirt, on which was traced a detailed map of half a square mile of the Outer Hebrides, and savagely wished myself there.

His worst failing so far is jealousy. The last time I rang him at the office, his secretary said earnestly, 'I haven't seen hare nor hound of him.' But if *he* rings *me* and I don't answer, there is likely to be an inquisition. Last week it got beyond a joke. I had taken the phone off the hook because Mr Pembleton had come round to give me my clarinet lesson and at nine pounds an hour I don't like to take any chances on being interrupted. Anyway, towards the end of the lesson we were deep into a passage of Albinoni, quite transported by its bosky rills, and Mr Pembleton's eyebrows were leaping in time to the rhythm as always, when in burst my bellowing pin-striped husband. It was very embarrassing. I was furious. Mr Pembleton was almost crying as he slunk off, not even given enough time to pack away his clarinet properly.

I shall have to be more careful in future.

Sometimes I have a dream that tears through me like a hurricane and leaves me shaking, the sort of dream that used to be explained away as the work of devils. There were sleepy female demons who gave out such heat that even in midwinter the soporific lettuce seeds sprouted when they walked by, the mere rustle of their skirts made frosty rosebushes blossom into full-blown crimson. Such a succuba would descend in a hot dream upon a sleeping man with an appetite so violent that by the time she had finished with him even the densest-bearded would wake quite exhausted and feeling as though his bones had been dislocated. My own hurri-canes would no doubt have been described as the work of that cocky male devil the incubus, whose nocturnal interference was held responsible for the births of mutants and monsters.

Occasionally, at the end of some mad sparkling quar-rel, he clubs me down at last with that spiteful threat: 'What *you* need is a baby. *That* would sort you out.' Oh yes, that would be the end of this road and no mistake. They're all on his side, of course: First, It was ordained for the procreation of children, etc.

Do you think it possible that a dream confluence – put it more bluntly, fusion with a chimera – might result in a phantom pregnancy? Or does the waking self give up the ghost?

My dreams have been with me from the edge of childhood, mostly the sort of dream in which every courtesy is maintained and every permission given; but I never knew before I married what it was to be a quarreller. Our rows are like the weather, there is no control over them and very little warning, sometimes none at all. We might be basking in the sunshine when a squall appears from nowhere and within seconds develops into a howling tornado. At the same time and with equal speed we hurtle back down the decades, transformed into giant infants stamping and frowning and spouting tears of rage.

'*Don't* talk to me then! See if I care!' rings out with playground simplicity.

I slap his arm and burst into tears of rage and disappointment. I follow him into the next room. 'What about the time you left me stranded by the Albert Memorial,' I yell.

'You sound just like a scratched old record,' he hisses. He follows me upstairs. Insults cramp my throat. I find the best one and aim it carefully like a dart. I watch the pupils disappear to pin-points in the great excited aquamarine irises of his eyes.

'Go away! Go away!' I shout, turning to the wall as he approaches and whamming my forehead against it.

Every time this happens I am astonished at the pack of devils let loose.

We fall into bed like two nasty children. He says things so hard that I feel little shooting spasms in sexual places, so then I feel they *must* be true. I am quiet. I think about them. Then I slap out at him and he thumps me, so I scratch and bite. He says my name after I've turned out the light but I don't answer. We lie awake in that sort of long dead silence when all future life is Arabia Deserta.

We still behave fairly normally in public, avoiding the little bitternesses which longer-established married couples automatically bat to and fro without self-consciousness. Recently we had to go to a dinner party given by one of my husband's grateful clients. Towards the end of the meal, the client's wife ran in from her kitchen bearing a Baked Alaska alight with blue rum-based flames. In case you don't know about Baked Alaska, it is a nightmare of a pudding which only a fool would try to make, a large lump of ice cream covered with heavily whipped sugar-stiffened raw egg-whites sitting on a sponge cake. This structure is cauterised in a scorching oven for three minutes, during which time the ice cream is supposed to stay frozen while the meringue bakes to brown peaks. It is what you might call the Ur-recipe for disaster.

The client and his wife were a fairly tense couple anyway, but the stealthy sniping with which they had seasoned the early part of the meal was now given culinary fulfilment.

'Knife, darling.' His voice rose to shrillness. '*Sharp* knife.'

'I *know*, darling, but cut it faster than you did last time,' she urged. 'You remember what happened *then*.'

'It's *melting*, darling,' he barked.

'You're not cutting it *fast* enough,' she said. A slice shot across the waiting tea-plate, and ice cream slopped onto the tablecloth.

'Come on, come *on*!' Her brows were knitting

furiously, and she was dancing a little jig at his side.

'It's been in too long,' he said as the second slice collapsed.

'Three minutes and not a second more, on my mother's grave,' she said with hatred. 'It's *you*. You're so *slow*.'

The table had fallen silent, no chit-chat being possible at the borders of such a scene. I looked on with what I thought of as a sort of Olympian compassion at first, until, like a tuning fork, I shuddered, catching certain unmistakably *married* reverberations.

This morning when I wolf-whistled him as he emerged shaggy and glistening from the shower, he clapped his hands over himself and said, 'That's not exactly very feminine, is it.' He has beautiful hands, fine as earth, rough and warm like brown sand. Sometimes he lets me wash his back and shoulders, which is when I get the *marvelling* feeling most strongly. I have never told him about this.

I first felt helpless admiration when I watched him come off the court after a game of tennis, pulling off his shirt as roughly as a child would, his sweat drops white and pearly in the sun. His face was brighter than silver, sunburnt to coppery patches on the cheekbones, his florid shoulders weathered almost to the colour of claret. Let me love you, I said silently as we went to bed that night for the first time, let me stroke your shadows with my fingers and inhale your skin's smell of honey and air; let me love you before you heave ho my hearty.

At night, in pyjamas (which did not appear until after the wedding), he curled to me like a striped mollusc, with the long curving back of a prawn. My little croco-dile, I said maliciously as he draped his length against me

9

in bed. When he whispered in my ears (which he still does sometimes) then he caused trembling while my fingers and toes turned to sparklers. It made him groan like a wood-pigeon before falling asleep, though usually I was chortling away for some time afterwards.

Then, my mind was a sunny prairie of contentment; my body was quick, god-like, with a central line of stars. There was the scarcely-dare-believe-it hope that marriage might even mean years of this ahead, safeguarding a life of such subterranean holiday in perpetuity. Yes, yes, there is more to marriage that *that*, I know that now; but surely there is nothing as good.

About six months ago, a week or two after the marrying event, we were walking along the edges of some stubbled corn-fields when we came to a solitary house in a field of its own. We looked through the windows — some of which were broken – and there was no furniture inside, so we didn't feel like intruders when we lifted the latch of the garden gate. Concealed by its hedge from the gaze of idle ramblers was a menagerie of topiary, wild-looking peacocks, boars sprouting long leafy green bristles, one or two blurred heraldic hounds. It was hot, late in the afternoon, and we lay down on a bed of box clippings at the end of the garden. I could see horse-chestnut trees nodding beyond the hedge. The densely knit noise of bees came from a nearby tangle of black-berries. I slipped out of my clothes, we lay together on his shirt, we concentrated suddenly for a while on a time of intense and escalating delight. Afterwards I was wicked with pleasure, and we shared the bread roll and apples saved from our pub lunch. I remember noticing the red and green striations on the apples' skins and the miraculous honey-combed structure of the bread. Then we fell asleep.

I dreamed an urgent heated dream of the sort which sometimes follows hard on the heels of satisfaction.

I was walking down the High Street in Bakewell with a modest strong young man. He was quite tall; as he talked to me, he turned his head slightly and tipped his glance down to shoulder level. He was telling me how he made all his own bread, how easy it was, just two or three loaves a week, or four when he felt unusually hungry.

'How on earth do you find the time,' I said. 'All that kneading and proving.'

'Oh, you can fit that in round other things in the odd few minutes here and there,' he assured me.

He showed me his current mass of dough, throwing it lightly from hand to hand like a goal-keeper. Then he wore it as a vast damp pliable boxing glove, deftly pulling at it and pummelling it with his other hand.

'You try,' he said. I found the glove-trick manipulation too difficult, so instead I kneaded away enthusiastically. It grew and grew, elastic and cirrus-streaked, until I felt worried.

'Have I spoiled the loaf?' I asked anxiously.

'Not at all,' he said. 'It'll be even better than usual.' We continued our walk, his arm round my shoulder as friendly as could be.

When I woke up it was almost evening, warm and still. I watched his crumpled face a foot away coming out of sleep, the lids flickering, light clearing the eyes and then a wreath of smiles.

We used to be *friends* then.

He upends me, he takes no notice of anything above the waist. How would *he* like it, that's what *I'd* like to know. And after some farmyard activity, while *I'm* still inside my nightdress, very often, he cages me in his big arms and legs and disappears with a snore.

'How did you sleep?' My husband has started to make casual enquiries. 'Did you have any interesting dreams?' I found a rubbishy paperback calling itself a Dictionary of Oneirology in his briefcase the other night when I was looking for *The Times*. How fascinating to learn that in Islam dreams of shrews are always related to faithless wives; I wonder if that works the other way around. And dreams of being infected with vermin are often the equivalent for pregnancy, it says here. No flies on *me*. Soon he will be cross-questioning me about the possible appearance of daggers, snakes, nail-files and umbrellas in my night pictures.

What does worry me is that I am finding it increasingly difficult to tell the difference between dreaming and awake. I often feel quite astonished when I turn out of a dream into the morning. I shout or laugh in dreams and wake my husband. I dream I am dreaming; or I dream I have woken up. I try to test whether a dream is a dream by cutting a plate of sardine sandwiches; I scoff the lot and am none the wiser. Recently I tried biting my hand in a dream to see if I was awake. Next morning there were toothmarks, so where does that leave me?

I was very late back one night last week, and crept up the stairs hoping he would have fallen asleep. No such luck. He was propped up against the pillows, and closed *Anna Karenina* with a bang as I came into the room.

'It took ages to find a taxi,' I said. 'They seem to dry up after eleven.'

'Why didn't you catch the train? The last one doesn't go until eleven-thirty.'

'I know, but Rhoda and I were having such an interesting discussion in the wine bar. The film was very thought-provoking.'

'What was it again?'

'*Battleship Potemkin*.' Surely he wouldn't have seen that. *I* certainly hadn't.

'Ah. What was it about?'

'Oh, you know, the nature of war, particularly at sea.'

'And you and Rhoda sat till past midnight discussing naval tactics over the Liebfraumilch.'

'Along with related matters. Look, you can just stop being so suspicious. I'm sick of your bullying. I'm going to get changed.' I stormed off to the bathroom with my nightdress.

'Stay here,' he called. No fear, I thought as I bolted the bathroom door. That way he would see that, at the particular request of Mr Pembleton, I had uncharacteristically left off my bra. I took a quick cold shower using Coal Tar soap, and went back into the bedroom with an innocent smile.

'Where did you find a taxi,' he said.

'Oh, don't start again.'

'I want to know.'

'Waterloo Bridge.'

'But you say you met Rhoda at the Barbican.'

'Yes, I did, but the wine bar was a little way off, and then there are no taxis in the City late at night. So we carried on walking because we knew there are always taxis on Waterloo Bridge.'

'It's miles to Waterloo from the Barbican.'

'I *know*, and that's why I'm so tired and cross and longing for bed. And if that's all the sympathy you can show, I wish I'd never married you.' I burst into tears at last, and finally convinced him of my blamelessness, so much so that he apologised and kissed me goodnight.

Then I woke up, and the crocodile tears were still trickling down my cheeks. I looked at the clock – five a.m. – and at the sleeping bulk beside me, remembering how we had spent the previous evening in front of the fire playing chess. You see how confusing it can be.

He beat me at that game of chess as he usually (though not invariably) does. When I was putting the pieces away, thinking about them one by one, I said, 'I like the knight best. I like his L-shaped hopping.'

'You would,' said my husband, *bitterly*. The funny thing was, I understood exactly how he felt.

When I catch him in some detail of his body, whirling his little finger round an ear rim or squeezing a pore on the wing of his nose, our eyes meet coldly and he looks away. These fugitive glimpses of hatred between us are frighteningly hearty.

Yesterday, on my way to the shops, I was standing waiting to cross at the busy corner by Marchmont Drive, when a blue plumber's van flew by. The driver's window was open and, although he must have been doing fifty, I caught a long moment of his burnished shoulder and beautiful naked arm with the underarm tuft like the beard of a mussel. There was a blast of music – 'Get Out of My Dream and Into My Car' – as potent as a rogue whiff of jasmine, then it was all gone. I almost cried; I still had a lump in my throat by the time I reached the dry-cleaners. You're not saying that means nothing.

Recently I have noticed a disturbing change. Disapproving of my keeping any secrets from him, my husband has started appearing at precisely the wrong moment in places where he doesn't belong. Last night I was lying in a tipped-back chair while the dentist puffed some sort of dizziness around me until I was only half-conscious. He approached and stroked me, removing his white coat, holding me, pressing me to him; and then my husband appeared in the doorway and said, 'Excuse me, I'll take over now.'

I woke furious to his unconscious weight at my side. I felt like hitting him, but subsided, snarling. When I got back again I was by the sea and it was warm luminous evening. The light was so rare, the sky and sea of such a strange icy blue-green, that I knew I was further north than usual. I walked a few steps along sibilant shingle and quietly plosive bladderwrack, noticing that both a red sun and a yellow moon were in the sky, though the sun was very low. Now, running lightly down the dunes of marram grass appeared some sort of fisherman or sea-gypsy; I was only able to take in the black eyes with their oblique gleam.

He was beside me and the sides of our faces touched; his felt like the skin of a starfish and mine like the lining of a shell. I was both aware of existing in my own body – the mild drumming of my pulses, the gentle maritime roar in my ears – and of being able to see myself and this other figure standing on the shore.

15

He took a small mother-of-pearl box from his trouser pocket and gave it to me, watching intently as I nodded my thanks. Then his arm lifted at the elbow and he slid his finger under a strand of hair which had stuck to my forehead. I saw my face and neck flood with colour just as the disappearing sun set fire to a stripe of sea. He slid his hand suddenly through the deep armhole of my dress and his fingers curled to the shape of my breast. I lost all power and was beached onto his shoulder.

Time makes a little leap. We are in a house built of driftwood and pine branches. The windows show oblongs of brine-blanched aquamarine; there are bubbles and knots in the glass. He is stoking the sea-coal fire. I stand waiting and hot salt tears brim up. He draws me gently into him again. I feel the extreme heat of his body; it radiates through his clothes like the sun. The middle of my own body bucks softly, gratefully. We stare at each other with reluctant half-smiles, and from our stiff breathing you might think we are about to fight.

We lie down together on the bed by the wall. I close my eyes, curiously at rest now, floating. His violent hand plucks me from my suspension in the middle air and I hug him with equal violence. We rock together as though it seems our ribs must crack.

But when at last it comes to it, clipped in the warm frame of his arms, thighs enfolded in his tangle, at this moment I happen to glance across his shoulder and so spoil everything. It has been going swimmingly but now there will be no conclusion. I sit up, spit words of refusal, glare across the room.

He has done it again. This second invasion *proves* he

has broken my cover. Now I will never more be private, even in the slumbering third part of my time. There at the window, his face like a censorious turnip, my husband is staring in.

Good Friday, 1663

We have a winding sheet in our mother's womb, which grows with us from our conception, and we come into the world, wound up in that winding sheet, for we come to seek a grave.

My rustic husband, preferring to be fifty years behind the times in church matters as in all else, has ordered Parson Snakepeace to preach only sermons from the old dead Divines, and to read them aloud without comment. This being Good Friday, he has chosen the horridest sermon he could find, all to do with death and earthworms.

Lord, I'm sure I am grown quite melancholy at that old barbarous tale of the thorn crown and the sponge in vinegar. Ha, ha, ha!

This church is as cold as the grave. You would not know the air was so gentle outside, all the daffodils kissing the air and the apple trees like brides.

19

Here, by my pew, lies my husband's mother, Myrtilla
Fanshawe, 26 years old, d. 1634, boxed up in fine Carrara:

God's goodness made her wise and well-beseeming
Her wifely virtues won her much esteeming,
Earth would not yield more pleasing earthly bliss
Blest w'two babes, though Death brought her to this.

That shallow space over there, beneath the window
showing St Catherine, is reserved for *my* tomb. I insist on
a chaste design. None of your beastly seraphim, mind; I
never could endure your marble flittermice.

Myrtilla died in childbed, bearing that blockhead my
husband. He sits beside me now pretending to listen to
the sermon, his mouth catching flies, a pure clown, mere
elementary earth, without the least spark of soul in him.
That he should have claimed *me* for his wife! He would
be more fitly mated with some silly, simple, peaking,
sneaking country girl, one that goes with her toes in, and
can't say boo to a goose.

I cannot endure him near me, with his sweating,
snoring, scratching, snap-finger ways. He'll sit and yawn,
and stretch like a greyhound by the fireside, till he does
some nasty thing or other and so gives me an excuse to
leave the room. When he has blown his nose into his
handkerchief, he looks into it as if there were a diamond
dropped out of his head.

**There in the womb we are fitted for works of
darkness, all the while deprived of light: and
there in the womb we are taught cruelty, by**

20

being fed with blood, and may be damned, though we be never born.

To confine a woman just at her rambling age! take away her liberty at the very time she should use it! O barbarous aunt! O unnatural father!

My aunt Champflower is a very violent lady. She will fall into a fit or fly at you for the least piddling insignificant thing. In her day she was a beauty, but now she washes her face and hands in lead varnish to hide the dismal hollows of eight and thirty years.

Lord, what a difference there is between me and her. How I should despise such a thing if I were a man. What a nose she has! what a chin! what a neck! She desired my ruin with all her little heart. She danced for pure joy at my wedding.

My father never would have heard Scandal's buzz had she only kept it from him. He would have let me look where I pleased for a husband. I have a tidy fortune. But, no, I must be thrown away in haste to this clodpoll squire.

My aunt calls me to her room and talks of Honour and Reputation with a long face like the beast of the Nile.

'Aye, aye,' says I, 'but what has such talk to do with me?'

'What indeed!' cries she in a passion.

She pauses. She trifles with a lace some time before she speaks next, making play with a certain letter, reading it to herself with a careless dropping lip and an erected brow, humming it hastily over.

I recognise the hand. It is from my Celadon.

'Well, niece, this galloping abroad and allowing young

fellows to fool with you has given your reputation no very good complexion.'

'Madam, I seek only to follow your example. Besides, I have heard it said often and often when I was with you in London, that a lady's reputation ought to be a sort of brunette; then it has an attraction in it, like amber. A white reputation is as disagreeable to men, I am sure I have heard you say twenty times or more, as white eyebrows or white eyelashes.'

'Pooh pooh,' says she with a sort of snarling smile. 'You can talk in that airy impertinent way until Domesday but it will not save you. I have other letters. Your fop delights in nothing but rapes and riots, as all the world well knows. I have heard certain tales. I have ocular proof.'

'Madam,' says I, though I start to feel a little uneasy now, 'there are some persons who make it their business to tell stories, and say this and that of one and t'other, and everything in the world; and,' says I . . .

'And your father shall know all,' she finishes.

Our birth dies in infancy, and our infancy dies in youth, and youth and the rest die in age, and age also dies, and determines all. O, huzza, Parson Snakepeace; cheerful matter for an April morning! **Our youth is hungry and thirsty, after those sins, which our infancy knew not; and our age is sorry and angry, that it cannot pursue those sins which our youth did.**

I shall never more see the playhouse, nor go to Ponchinello nor Paradise, nor take a ramble to the Park nor

Mulberry Garden. I could as soon persuade my husband to share a sillybub in New Spring Garden or to drink a pint of wine with friends at the Prince in the Sun as I could fly.

My aunt Champflower took me with her to London last year for a spring holiday. We lodged near by St James's, and I never was so happy in all my life.

I dote upon assemblies, adore masquerades, my heart bounds at a ball; I love a play to distraction, cards enchant me, and dice put me out of my little wits.

On our third evening, then, we saunter to the pleasure gardens at Vauxhall for the sake of the Chinese lanterns and to taste a dish of oysters.

There we happen to meet again with a certain merry sharking fellow about the town, who has pursued us diligently from chocolate house to milliner to the Haymarket since our arrival. He has with him a friend; and this friend is Celadon.

'I came up, sir, as we country-gentlewomen use, at an Easter Term,' explains my aunt demurely, 'to the destruction of tarts and cheesecakes, to see a new play, buy a new gown, take a turn in the Park, and so down again to sleep with my forefathers.'

'We see you have brought your sister with you in kindness,' says Celadon, giving me a mighty wink.

The two fine gallants pay her gross and lavish compliments, ogling and glancing and watching any occasion to do forty officious things. They have all the appearance of gentlemen about them. I notice that Celadon's eyes look sideways on me like an Egyptian drawing. He wears a fine long periwig tied up in a bag.

My aunt curtseys at last. Down goes her diving body

to the ground, as if she were sinking under the conscious load of her own attractions; then launches into a flood of fine language, still playing her chest forward in fifty falls and risings, like a swan upon waving water.

Hang me if she has not conceived a violent passion for the fellow.

. . . when my mouth shall be filled with dust, and the worm shall feed, and feed sweetly upon me, when the ambitious man shall have no satisfaction, if the poorest alive tread upon him, nor the poorest receive any contentment in being made equal to Princes, for they shall be equal but in dust.

I look down now at my arms and see the fine eggshell skin with a pretty sparkle from the sun, and the violet-coloured veins at my wrist. I cannot think I am dust and worms' meat.

The carnation dew, the pouting ripeness of my honeycomb mouth, he said; and that my face was a swarm of cupids.

I do love Love, I would have all the Love in the world. What should I mind else, while I have any share of youth and beauty? When I went to Court all eyes were upon me, all tongues were whispering that's my Lord Spatchcock's fine daughter; all pressed towards me and bowed, only to get half a glance from me. When I went to the playhouse, some stood gazing on me, with their arms across their heads languishing as oppressed by beauty. The brisker fellows combed their wigs and prepared their eyes to tilt with mine. Ah, flattery was my daily bread.

24

Celadon is so agreeable a man, so eloquent, so unaffected, so particular, so easy, so free. All his finery is from the best in Paris, his shoes from Piccar and his gloves from Orangerie. He wears his clothes with so becoming a negligence that I can barely wish him out of them.

He had the greatest skill in arranging assignations that ever I saw; and all the while he flattered my aunt with a thousand honeyed words and promises, until I was ready to burst with laughing.

My hair was dressed in flaunting little ringlets and crimped serpentaux puffs. I wore my new under-petticoats of white dimity, embroidered like a turkey-work chair with red, green, blue and yellow, with a pin-up coat of Scotch plaid adorned with bugle lace and my gown of printed calico.

I carried my claret-coloured velvet coat with gold fringes to protect me from the dangers of the night air. Even in spring, jaunting abroad at four in the morning strikes a chill into the bones.

Parson Snakepeace has conceived the pretty notion of keeping a skull upon his desk.

I can never persuade myself that religion consists in scurvy out-of-fashion clothes and sour countenances, and when one walks abroad, not to turn one's head to the right or left, but hold it straight forward like an old blind mare.

O that I were your lover for a month or two, he murmured in my ear like a bumble bee.

– What then?

– I would make that pretty heart's blood of yours ache in a fortnight.

25

**That God, this Lord, the Lord of life could die,
is a strange contemplation; that the Red Sea
could be dry, that the sun could stand still,
that an oven could be seven times heat and not
burn, that lions could be hungry and not bite,
is strange, miraculously strange, but super-
miraculous that God could die.**

The most unnatural spectacle to be seen in Somerset
since the Flood was surely my union with Squire Clodpoll here. A dainty girl of seventeen yoked to a greasy,
untoward, ill-natured, slovenly wretch! We were the
laughing stock of five counties.

Now it is five months since our wedding, which I
should rather call a show of Merry-Andrews, with
nothing pleasant about it at all but the foolery of a farce.

The nuptial banquet was crammed with baskets of
plum-cake, Dutch gingerbread, Cheshire cheese, Naples
biscuits, macaroons, neats' tongues and cold boiled beef.

My new husband had drunk heartily. The guests cried
out for a speech. He staggered to his feet.

My head aches consumedly, said he; I am not well.

He raised his glass to me, then toppled over behind the
table.

There was such a laughing, they roared out again. The
ladies teehee'd under their napkins. The teehee took a
reverend old gentlewoman as she was drinking, and she
squirted the beer out of her nose, as an Indian does
tobacco.

By the time the bashful bride, meaning myself, was
brought to bed, this numbskull had in some wise
recovered his wits. He called for a mouthful of something

to stay his stomach, a tankard of usquebaugh with nutmeg and sugar, if you please, and also a toast and some cheese.

'Supper, sir!' said I. 'Why, your dinner is not out of your mouth yet; at least 'tis all about the brims of it.'

That sharp comment confounded him, so that he cursed, and rolled about the bedchamber like a sick passenger in a storm; then he comes flounce into bed, dead as a salmon in a fishmonger's basket, his feet cold as ice and his breath hot as a furnace.

His head is a fool's egg which lies hid in a nest of hair. He hangs his nose in my neck and talks to me whether I will or no. What a poor sordid slavery there is in the state of marriage.

During our brief courtship, he wailed out some songs of love.

> *I have a mistress that is fair*
> *And as sweet as sugar candy,*
> *Had I ten thousand pounds a year*
> *I'd give her half a pint of brandy.*

And all the while he gazes on me like a sick monster, with languishing eyes.

I burst into laughter: 'Lord, sir, you have such a way with you, ha, ha, ha!'

At night He went into the garden to pray, and He spent much time in prayer. I dare scarce ask thee whither *thou* wentest, or how *thou* disposedst of thy self, when it grew dark and

after last night. That has set my husband a-tittering. Now he nudges me with his elbow, the filthy fellow. I have no stomach for him. **About midnight He was taken and bound with a kiss, art thou not too conformable to Him in that? Is not that too literally, too exactly thy case? at midnight to have been taken and bound with a kiss?**

Yes, yes, Parson Snakepeace, I was taken captive in a garden, at my Lady Wildsapte's last summer *fête champestre*, though I cannot see why you should make a sermon of it, for it had nothing to do with you or your talk of the grave.

We went chasing off by the light of torches down an alley of trees, shamming to fight each other with long hazel twigs.

My lady's grounds are full of little pagan temples and other fancies, and at last we fell down breathless at the foot of a pretty Egyptian obelisk brought back by her son from his late stay in Rome. Screened by the friendly shade of some low bushes, we fell upon the ground together; the leaves around us were of the crimson flowering currant for I can still recall the sharp smell when we bruised 'em by lying upon 'em.

'Cherubimical lass,' he called me, and gazed on me devouringly. Our eye beams were in that moment tangled beyond redemption, and I could not bring myself to draw away when he caught me by the hand, wringing and squeezing at it as if he were mad.

He offered me no other rudeness at first, but we only gazed on each other with half smiles; and our breathing grew laboured when we twisted and knotted our fingers together as if in combat. Then indeed my bounding blood beat quick and high alarms.

He swore that he would come down from London in a fortnight, and marry me.

And so we progressed until, with broken murmurs and heart-fetched sighs, he so mousled and tousled me that I cried, 'Sweetheart!' and he clapped a hand over my mouth to save us from discovery.

Good gods! What a pleasure there is in doing what we should not do.

Then were we animated by the strongest powers of love, and every vein of my body circulated liquid fires; until we came at last to that tumultuous momentary rage of which so much has been whispered since the world began.

O Jesu, when I think back to the heat of his sweet mouth and the smell of his skin, I could weep for weeks together.

Hang him, let him alone. He's gone.

Hast thou gone about to redeem thy sin, by fasting, by Alms, by disciplines and mortifications, in the way of satisfaction to the Justice of God? that will not serve, that's not the right way, we press an utter crucifying of that sin that governs thee; and that conforms thee to Christ.

Well, I am eight months gone with child. I may follow Mrs Myrtilla's example more speedily than expected. That would indeed be a convenient conclusion, to be

29

dispatched by my own sin. That would provide matter enough for a month of fine long thundering sermons.

This husband sits beside me like a ball and chain. A pack of squalling infants will do the rest, forging my bonds link by link, and soon I shall inhabit as heavy a carcass as my sister Sarah's. Then will I keep company with the mid-wife, dry-nurse, wet-nurse, and all the rest of their accomplices, with cradle, baby-clouts and bearing clothes – possetts, caudles, broth, jellies and gravies. I grow nauseous when I think of them.

I may build castles in the air, and fume and fret, and grow pale and ugly, if I please; but nothing will bring back my free and airy time.

Outside this church it is almost summer; see how the sun struggles through these coloured glass saints to fall in jewels onto my gown.

I will not die of the pip, so I will not.

O merciful God, who hast made all men, and hatest nothing that thou hast made, nor wouldest the death of a sinner, but rather that he should be converted and live; have mercy upon all Jews, Turks, infidels, and Hereticks, and take from them all ignorance, hardness of heart, and contempt of thy Word; and so fetch them home, blessed Lord, to thy flock, that they may be saved among the remnant of the true Israelites, and be made one fold under one shepherd, Jesus Christ our Lord, who liveth and reigneth with thee and the Holy Spirit, one God, world without end. Amen.

Give Me Daughters Any Day

'Does he *have* to be here?' said her grandmother. 'It's not right, having a man in the house when I'm ill.'

'He does live here,' said Ruth. 'We're married, you see.'

'Call that a man,' said her grandmother. 'He's back by five o'clock. He doesn't even teach a proper subject. We all know *English!* He's no use. Look at the handle on that door, it's hanging half off. Why doesn't he fix it?'

'We haven't been here long,' said Ruth. 'We're doing things gradually.'

'Gradually!' jeered her grandmother.

'Can I make you some more tea?' asked Ruth coldly. 'Only I've got to get on otherwise.'

'Oh yes, your *job*. Why don't you make that husband of yours get a *proper* job, a *man*'s job. He's *limp*.'

'Women don't like only doing housework and having babies these days,' said Ruth. 'We want to be independent and fulfilled too.'

31

'You do talk a lot of rubbish,' said her grandmother. 'Just like your mother. She made a fool of that man, cooking him casseroles and buying him Shetland jumpers. Didn't stop him leaving though, did it. *You'd* better watch out for that.'

'I'm not staying in this room if you won't be polite.'

'Suit yourself. You're not doing *me* any favours. I don't *want* to be here, I was made to come. I wish I'd never agreed. I want my own things. I *hate* this house.'

'I know, I know,' said Ruth. 'I don't blame you. But you know what Dr Singh said. The alternative is hospital.'

'Oh, doctors,' said her grandmother, and lapsed back onto the sofa-bed, grey-yellow hair awry on the candy-striped pillows. 'Your ceiling looks like the icing on a wedding cake,' she continued, gazing upwards with gooseberry-coloured eyes.

'She wants you to stay out of her room,' said Ruth to Denzil.

'But all my clothes are in there!'

'Well, I'll have to bloody well get them out,' said Ruth.

'There's a strong Anglo-Saxon element in your family,' said Denzil. 'Your language. Your grandmother's gnomic utterances. "We all have dustbins for minds, but some of us prefer to keep the lids on." "You've got a son until he marries but you keep a daughter for life." As for that spare room now ... Did you ever hear of Grendel's cave?'

'No. And don't do that. I'm too tired.'

Denzil let her go.

'Do you know what she said to me this evening when I asked her how she was?' he said after a while. 'She said, "I'm feeling a little queer but I suppose I mustn't grouse."'

'Why did I get married?' said Ruth.

'Not that again,' said Denzil, leafing through his Dictionary of Historical Slang. 'Queer, adjective. Base; criminal, from sixteenth century. Derivative senses, drunk, 1800, hence unwell, giddy, from 1810.'

'She says *you're* queer because you're called Denzil,' said Ruth.

'Does she,' said Denzil. 'That's rich, coming from someone called Vesta. Grouse. Cognate with the old French groucier. From 1850, dialect, to grumble.'

'She said there was nothing she could fancy except boiled tongue,' continued Ruth with a bitter laugh. 'So I found a tongue in that smelly old butchers down by the station but when I got it back and read the recipe it said I had to skin it and put it under heavy weights for hours and hours. It was very expensive too.'

'Tongue,' said Denzil. 'Can't you buy it by the pound at Cullens?'

'I *tried* that. She said it tasted wrong.'

'What do you want me to do, then? Have a go at skinning it?'

'Don't bother. She's had pints of Slippery Elm so she won't starve. Wrap the damn thing up in newspaper and take it out to the dustbin.'

'Couldn't we give it to someone?' asked Denzil uneasily. 'Seems a waste.'

'You bloody well cook it then!' yelled Ruth, tears spurting from the corners of her eyes in jets. 'I haven't been able to do any of *my* work. You're all right, colouring in your third-year charts with pretty crayons, but my agency is grinding to a standstill before it's even got off the ground and much *you* care.'

'Modern men,'croaked Denzil. 'They're all the same. Dirty rotten lot.'

'And don't sneer,' wept Ruth. 'You patronising git.'

Ruth was in the process of setting up the Little Bo Peep Agency for baby-minders and nannies. She had allowed this month to check up on local council regulations and to write an emergency information sheet to distribute among the less experienced of her team.

'Projectile vomiting,' she copied out from a baby manual. 'Do not be alarmed. This is not too serious. Clear up the wall, and inform the mother on her return.'

She took up a tray of tea.

'What have you been up to?' said Vesta.

'I've been trying to write a leaflet but I don't think it's any good.'

'You've been wasting your time, then, haven't you,' Vesta said, incontrovertibly.

'I think I'll try and work here for a bit,' said Ruth, and brought out her book.

'Always bloody well reading,' said Vesta, glaring at the wardrobe. 'First your mother, now you. And if it's not the books, it's some mad scheme or other. *Never* any money, either. Your mother's never had two pennies to rub together. Look at the state of her flat. I wouldn't be seen dead in it. At least you live in a house. Of sorts.'

Ruth tried to concentrate on the print in front of her

eyes. 'It is important to teach the child basic principles of "do as you would be done by". It may seem obvious to you that it is wrong to scream your head off when thwarted. It is not obvious to a very young child.'

'What are you reading?' asked Vesta.

'A book on babies so I can write a leaflet for my Bo Peep Agency.'

'What a damnfool name that is,' said Vesta. 'And a damnfool idea too. What do *you* know about babies? You've never had any.'

'You don't always have to experience things personally to know about them.'

'You've left it a bit late in the day if you're thinking of having one now. Even if you did, you'd have *old* babies. Wizened little things with all sorts of problems.'

'I'm only thirty and I'm *not* thinking of having one now,' said Ruth. 'Time enough when I've got some money coming in from Little Bo Peep.'

'I wouldn't bother if I were you,' said Vesta. 'They're more trouble than they're worth. I never had anything but trouble from Janet.'

'But mum's been visiting you every fortnight since grandad died,' said Ruth. 'And that was over twenty-five years ago.'

'Only because she's a social worker,' spat Vesta.

'She says we'll have old babies,' fretted Ruth that night in bed.

'We won't have *any* babies if you carry on setting your cap at me,' said Denzil.

'Don't try to make jokes,' said Ruth. 'Anyway, you

agreed it's more sensible like this until you get a Scale Two.'

'Oh yes,' he said. 'More sensible.'

'Why do you make me out to be such a killjoy?' asked Ruth.

'Sweetheart, nothing could be further from my mind,' said Denzil. 'But, if the cap fits.'

'You could always bugger off,' said Ruth. 'See if I care.'

'How are you feeling?' asked Ruth.

'Need you ask?' croaked Vesta.

'Here's the *Mail*,' said Ruth, 'And here are your glasses.'

'Have a cup of tea with me,' said Vesta. 'Look, you've made a ridiculous big pot, I can't drink all that by myself. When I see the waste that goes on in this house I don't wonder you're as poor as church-mice.'

'All right, I'll have a cup,' said Ruth. 'But I've got to make some phone calls this morning.'

'I'm not stopping you,' said Vesta. 'Did you go out for my *Mail* again? You shouldn't have to do that. Why can't you get it delivered? You must live in a very poor area. You should see my paper girl. She's the sexiest little devil you ever saw. It's disgusting really. Ginger hair, too. I wonder why it always goes with ginger?'

'*I've* got auburn hair,' said Ruth.

'You've let yourself go,' said Vesta dismissively. 'No make-up. Just scraping your hair back. Tell me when you get divorced, won't you. Not that *he's* much to write home about either.'

'Why don't you read your paper,' said Ruth, picking

36

up her copy of *Baby Management*. Her grandmother glared at her through her sharp-cornered reading glasses, then studied the headlines.

'Students again,' she muttered. 'Education's a dirty word. Look at the Communists, they've all been to University. That's why your husband won't get a proper job. All those ideas he got at University *sapped* him.'

'Oh, *shut* up,' said Ruth.

'You've got no control over him,' shouted Vesta. 'You can't even get him to put on a bloody door-handle.'

'Have a betablocker,' said Ruth coldly. 'If you've finished your breakfast.'

In the old days, Ruth had been sent by her mother during the school holidays to be company for her widowed grandmother.

Every morning they went shopping locally in Mortlake, with Ruth carrying the zip-up vinyl bag, for half a pound of this and a quarter of that. On the way they might meet one of Vesta's neighbours, and there would be a formal five-minute exchange on the subject of physical deterioration, while Ruth stood to one side, staring at the pavement. The conversation over, she followed her grandmother off again with mortified canine obedience. Their main meal, at midday, of chops or offal or stew, was followed by Vesta's Rest.

Ruth sat on the rug in the sun and filled in her diary. *'Je suis avec ma grandmère,'* she wrote. *'Ce soir nous donnerons le poisson au chat de Mme Grayling, qui est au Minorca en vacances. Hier soir nous avons entendu Radio 2 depuis deux heures et joué aux cartes. Je suis absolument . . .'*

37

She paused and bit her biro. What was she, absolutely?

She gave up and started to read, alternating chapters of *Mansfield Park* with *Forever Amber*. At about four, she went back to the kitchen and laid the tea things. She was in a hot trance of reading and wanted never to speak again.

At ten past four her grandmother came downstairs.

'Always got your nose in some damn book,' she said. 'What are you reading *now*?'

'At Mansfield,' Ruth read aloud, 'no sounds of contention, no raised voice, no abrupt bursts, no tread of violence was ever heard; all proceeded in a regular course of cheerful orderliness.'

'How boring,' said Vesta. 'I like a bit of life. Why can't you put that down and be *company*.'

'I've got to revise,' said Ruth.

'Don't think exams will get you anywhere,' laughed Vesta. 'Look where they got your mother. Spending her time with drug addicts and sex maniacs and the scum of the earth. No wonder that rotten husband of hers upped and offed.'

'You mustn't talk like that about my father,' said Ruth.

'I'll say what I want in my own house,' huffed Vesta. 'He was a lazy, dirty good-for-nothing. It's no surprise *he* ended up in the gutter.'

'I won't listen!' shrieked Ruth.

'You're getting absolutely neurotic,' said Vesta with distaste.

From the top of the kitchen dresser she pulled down her own favourite book, *The Pageant of Life* by Dr Ethel Tensing, 1931.

38

'You listen to this and you'll learn a thing or two,' said Vesta, looking at Ruth severely over her reading glasses.

'Oh, no, please,' said Ruth.

'Don't be so ignorant,' said Vesta. 'Now this is her chapter on Adolescence.' She proceeded to read aloud the opinions of half a century ago on subjects as various as menstruation and the advisability of excess energy being channelled into a hobby.

'You could try stamp collecting,' chuckled Vesta.

'I don't need a hobby,' said Ruth. 'I've got reading. And as far as I can see everything's just the same now I'm fifteen as when I was seven. I still go to school. I still come here every holiday.'

'Don't be so stupid,' said Vesta. 'You have your periods now, don't you.'

'Shut up, shut up, shut up,' said Ruth.

'The young adult, or adolescent, is particularly suscep-tible to unreasonable emotional swings,' Vesta read aloud.

'I'm going to be sick,' said Ruth, 'If you don't shut up. And you can't pronounce menstruation or comparable.'

'When are you going to get a boyfriend,' said Vesta.

'When am I going to meet any boys,' said Ruth.

'It's not natural,' said Vesta. 'Maybe it's because of your weight. But don't think you're going to help matters by trying to wear lipstick. That cheap stuff you put on yesterday made your lips look like two pieces of liver.'

'Shut up, shut up, shut up,' said Ruth, her voice higher this time.

'Calming breathing exercises for adolescents,' read

Vesta. 'Come on, now. Inhale deeply, filling the diaphragm with air.'

'You don't sound the *g*,' snivelled Ruth.

Fifteen years later Ruth was saying, 'No. Leave me alone.'

'Why?' said Denzil, breathing hard. 'It's her, isn't it.'

'Oh, go to sleep,' said Ruth. 'It's gone midnight. We're both tired.'

'Don't talk to me like that.'

'Like *what*.'

'Like I'm nothing.'

'You're not nothing,' said Ruth. 'Anyway, you can't. I've started.'

'I don't mind, if you don't,' said Denzil.

'I do mind,' said Ruth.

'Actually, I couldn't give a toss whether you do or not,' said Denzil, pushing his face into hers so that their teeth clashed.

'You're just selfish,' she hissed as they wrestled around on the bed. 'You come in at five o'clock, miles earlier than other men, and you sit around with your bits of paper while I'm up and down stairs with her bloody lemon barley water and rice pudding and pots of tea . . .'

'She won't *let* me go into her room,' interrupted Denzil.

'. . . And it's all very comfortable for you but I have to do everything and now my agency will be late starting if it ever starts and we'll never have enough money to carry on with the mortgage on this horrible house.'

'It's not a horrible house. You only say that because *she* said so.'

'I know,' she said. 'I know, I know.'

Back in the past, Ruth and her mother had visited Mortlake every other Saturday during term-time. Vesta was always spoiling for a fight after a fortnight on her own.

First, there was tea in the kitchen, the kettle smoking like the muzzle of a gun.

'Heard from that husband of yours lately?' said Vesta. This was her favourite opening gambit.

'Not for a while, no,' said Janet, bristling. 'Why?'

'Ha,' grunted Vesta with a merry look.

'What's *that* supposed to mean?' said Janet, humiliation transforming her features.

'Don't quarrel about Dad,' said Ruth. 'We've only just got here.'

'And *you* can shut up,' said Vesta equably, while Janet pulled out a crossword puzzle with a pitiable show of indifference.

The talk trundled off down the same old tracks, stale grudges revived and gathering impetus with the freshening of vicious memories. Soon it was rocketing along. Vesta's blood was up, her face was red. Janet was shouting hoarsely. Vesta was giving her best scornful laugh. Janet, panting, was in retreat, trying to recall her Mrs-Miniver-under-pressure face. Ruth was half way through the packet of Digestives, making a bet with herself about not grizzling before lunch.

'What are *you* looking like that for?' called her mother, with deflected bellicosity.

'I wish you two wouldn't fight,' mumbled Ruth.

There was a pause.

'You ought to speak to that girl,' said Vesta.

'I'll thank you not to interfere,' said Janet to Ruth.

'Why can't you be *nice* to each other,' whined Ruth.

'Your mother and I are very close,' said Vesta with dignity. 'We just rub each other up the wrong way sometimes.'

'Take no notice of her,' said Janet. 'She gets like this.'

'Ginger, too. Shame she takes after her father,' said Vesta, starting the ball rolling again.

By the end of her second week on the sofa-bed, Vesta had improved enough to dress and come down for her evening meal.

Janet had driven over after work and now crouched, flinching nervously like a horse attacked by flies, on a kitchen stool. Ruth, remorselessly silent, prepared the greens.

'What a day I've had,' said Janet brightly. 'First a schoolgirl mum, trying to persuade her to go back to school. Then a ten-year-old who put his mother in hospital last week. And a really sad case this afternoon, a nice old boy who can't cope on his own any more. A nasty fall he'd had this time, lying on his own there for two days. Incontinent too. We've done what we can but he'll have to go into a home.'

'Do shut up, mum,' said Ruth.

Looking wounded, Janet took out her cigarettes.

'Oh yes, your daughter's bossy all right,' said Vesta with an angry smile. 'You're looking dreadful, Janet. Your face is all drawn and haggard, and your mouth looks sunk in. That haircut does nothing for you. As for the dye, it makes you look like an old prostitute.'

'Well, thanks very much,' said Janet, turning a gaze of dog-like appeal on her daughter.

'It's the menopause, of course,' said Vesta with relish. 'When you stop being able to have children, your body gives up. You're no use any more. Your hair gets thin. Your skin goes dull. And then, you abuse your health, Janet, you always have. You live out of tins.'

Ruth caught herself glancing appraisingly, almost assessingly, at her mother. She turned to Vesta and said, 'You don't look so hot yourself.'

'What do you expect when you get to eighty-five,' said Vesta. In the last week her skin had acquired a translucent mulberry-coloured glaze, and her hands and arms had begun to look pollarded.

Ruth saw that her meal would be ready in a couple of minutes.

'Mum, I think you'd better go soon,' she said briskly. 'You're not doing much good here, and I'm just about to serve up.'

Vesta's eyes reddened and filled with tears. Janet stared at her daughter reproachfully.

Ruth watched them in disbelief. She put the frying pan down and walked out of the kitchen. When she came back, Janet had left.

'What was the matter then?' she asked.

'You were rude to your mother,' said Vesta tremulously. 'She thinks the world of you, and I didn't like it.'

'Phew,'said Denzil, twisting Ruth's left arm behind her back. 'You've become very aggressive in the last couple of weeks.'

They continued to grapple on the moonlit bed, growing increasingly hot and violent.

'Call yourself a man,' hissed Ruth. 'When are you going to get round to fixing that bloody door-handle.' She banged him on the ear. 'Limp, that's what you are,' she continued. 'University *sapped* you. Why don't you get yourself a proper job.'

'Right,' said Denzil, 'If you must.' He kicked her lightly but strategically, and they fell like trees onto the mattress.

'Limp, am I,' muttered Denzil.

'Very funny,' hissed Ruth.

Some while afterwards, Ruth said, 'Of course, you know what I forgot to do before we did that.'

Denzil smirked, his hot face inches from hers.

'Which do you think it'll be?' he muttered.

'Shut up, shut up, shut up,' said Ruth.

'Let's hope it's not a girl,' he continued. 'You can have too much of a good thing.'

Ruth pulled away from him. She knelt naked on the bed. The moon shone in.

'That's what I like,' said Denzil. 'Good child-bearing hips, too.'

Hands clenched, knuckles silver against her belly, Ruth began to knead inwards and downwards.

'No,' she said. 'No. No. *No.*'

44

The Bed

Let me tell you how a piece of furniture changed my life.
I had just moved into a flat with Tom, but things were
not going so well. We were poor and over-tired, the flat
was dark, dirty and sparsely furnished. I could not see
how it might get any better.

I had taken to wandering round department stores in
my lunch hour, soothed by the acquisitive absorption of
other women and by the somnambulistic glide of the
escalators. One day I found myself in the bedding department, a hushed and unpopulated area. I stood sur-
rounded by beds like Ruth waist-high amid the corn, and
was filled with a longing more poignant even than
homesickness. A rich meadow of sprigged brocade and
velvet padding stretched as far as the eye could see. The
beautiful mattresses absorbed all sound on this, the fifth
floor, and so I did not hear the footsteps of the Bedding
Manager.

'Can I help you, madam?' said the voice at my ear. I

turned and smiled. I did not need to think before I spoke. Consideration did not enter into it. It was an act of pure instinct.

'Yes, please. I want the best bed money can buy.'

Without worrying, which is unusual for me, I had taken the day off work to wait in for the bed. It was dark November, and the rain drummed tirelessly on the windows all day. I waited quietly, marvelling at how gloomy the light was in every room, without, however, minding about it. The colour of the air suited the portentous nature of this particular day. The bed arrived late in the afternoon, and I watched with jealous eyes as the men unloaded it, noticing immediately the wet corner frame where they had allowed its plastic covering to fall open. Rainwater does not stain, I told myself, and the mattress itself is dry as a bone, which is the important thing.

I followed the men upstairs as they lugged the folded bed-frame, crackling in its plastic bag. We reached the low-ceilinged part at last, the crooked approach to the bedroom door. The older man heaved and juggled for a few seconds, then turned his rain-streaked face to me.

'It won't go,' he said flatly.

'No. I don't believe you,' I replied.

'Nah, we'll have to take it back,' he persisted. 'Unless you've got a saw?'

I gaped at him, then realised this was his idea of a joke.

Together we assembled the bed. It stood as high as a horse, in layers like a mille-feuille slice, an enormous square of magnificence covered in creamy flowered satin. The little room looked shame-faced around it, like a flimsy shoe box. Next door's radio chattered on, clearly audible through the party wall.

'Nice bed,' commented the younger of the two, gazing at it, smiling with innocent pleasure.

Tom was not so happy. He grew white-hot and enraged, unable to believe that I had done this, furious, incoherent, his tie crooked and his suit steaming damply as we stood by the gas fire. I kept quiet while he let rip and hurled himself around the room.

'How the hell did you pay for it?' he snarled.

'Interest-free credit over ten months,' I mumbled. He smacked his forehead and gave a howl.

'£1,000!' he shouted. 'That's £100 a month, you realise! I suppose you think I should chip in?'

'Don't bother,' I said. 'I'll manage the money somehow.'

'Sponging off me!' he sneered. 'That's what it comes down to, isn't it? All your wonderful talk of independence.'

'You'll like sleeping in that bed too,' I said. I started to cry.

'You make me sick. It's the most irresponsible thing I ever heard of,' he said, and slammed the door behind him.

The flat wasn't really big enough for such scenes. If you left the sitting-room in this fine style, there was only the little bedroom or bathroom in which to cool down. Tom scorned these and stormed out into the rain, still in his suit. I thought of following him as he had had nothing to eat and was soaked through and tired out, but instead I went to have another look at the bed.

We had been sleeping on one of those hard, cheap,

Japanese-style mattresses called futons, stuffed with cotton wadding, claimed by the men who sold them to be good for your back. I hated it. It was so hard and ungiving that I felt bruised every morning when I woke up. The softer roundnesses of my body felt snubbed by it. Those futons might be all right for lean male athletes and ascetics, but I could never come to friendly sleeping terms with one of them.

I sat on the edge of my new, hand-upholstered, foot-deep, sprung-edge mattress, and realised how tired I was too. I rolled my head gently, easing the neck muscles, hearing the interior crunch of vertebrae. We had had another quarrel the night before. Tom had humped his back into a foetal arch and prepared, breathing slow and stertorous, to fall asleep with his usual ease. My mind had been alight and leaping with grievances. I could not rest. All issues of grief were sharp-edged and clamorous, jumping up in turn like rows of jack-in-the-boxes. I had wanted him to browse the pastures of insomnia with me, and was pleased when my restlessness prevented him from sleeping. The intensity of my sadness had been out of all proportion to its causes, which after all had only had their nourishment from everyday behaviour in its less attractive aspect. I had been forced up by a spasm of sleeplessness, running through the dark to the door, thudding in bare feet along the black alley to the front room. There I had fallen on the carpet and wept the sort of tears which leave the eyelids speckled with red to the brow next morning. Some time in the early hours I had returned to his side, thoroughly defeated, for some warm touch to banish the energetic mental banshees. And

48

when the morning came, four hours later, every conten-
tious issue was there clear as daylight as soon as I opened
my eyes, not ameliorated but no longer appalling.

When Tom returned, I did not rush out from the
bedroom for the further effort involved in any sort of
exchange between us. I tucked some clean sheets where
I could on the bed – they seemed ridiculously small
suddenly against the glossy acreage of the mattress – and
curled naked there under an eiderdown. I could hear
Tom moving angrily from room to room, but tonight it
was I who was the indifferent slumbering monarch. I
sank gratefully into an unbounded cradle of sleep. He did
not join me but I did not know that until eleven the next
morning, when I woke, fresh and sound and dreamless,
after an unbroken dozen hours of oblivion.

I glimpsed the clock and saw the broad light of late
morning, but felt none of the panic I would normally
experience on oversleeping on so grand a scale. I
stretched slowly until I tingled to the tips of my fingers
and toes. I felt well and strong and placid. I padded to
the kitchen and made a jug of coffee before ringing the
office to say that I was ill and would not be in. I took my
coffee back to bed with me, and lay there all day, smiling
and drowsing, stretching and smiling, without a practical
thought in my head. Tom was right, the bed and I were
in a happy alliance of irresponsibility.

He returned at seven that evening with some late
anemones and a bottle of wine.

'You shouldn't be looking so well and cheerful,' he
said, standing at the foot of the bed, grinning in spite of
himself, shrugging himself out of his suit.

'Come and get warm in here,' I said, and held out my

49

new sleep-strong arms to him. Legs wound together, arms straining tight, we made love with violent ease. Our bed bore us up like boats on water, buoyant, pliant and entirely silent.

Hot and happy, he turned his sly-smiling face to me.

'Well, it's a damn good bed for one thing, anyway,' he said.

We had slept in a fair number of beds during the two years we had been together, and each had presented its own unique difficulties. The one in Camberwell had been a worn-out shadow of a bed, rolling us down every night like rain water into a gutter. It had also been mounted on spitefully efficient castors, which meant that any movement more vigorous than turning one's head on the pillow would send it careering towards the wardrobe with prudish vehemence. In the house in Wood Green our room had had two single iron bedsteads which clanked in desolation. The landlady was an ex-matron, and these were ex-hospital beds. We lay side by side at night holding hands across the divide like characters in some terrible play by Samuel Beckett.

Beds are no fit matter for ridicule, no more than sleep or love. I have always liked the fairy-tale about the princess who proves the blueness of her blood by displaying the most exquisite sensitivity in her sleep.

'I trust you slept well, my dear?' enquires the cunning old Queen, laughing up her sleeve; under the twenty mattresses and twenty eiderdown quilts she has planted a pea.

'Oh, miserably!' replies the exhausted princess. 'I scarcely closed my eyes all night long. I lay upon something hard, so that I am black and blue all over.'

What can the sleep-depriving Queen do but allow her son to marry this girl who has shown such entirely proper delicacy over sleep?

Within a month of the bed's arrival, Tom acknowledged its worth and apologised for his initial hostility. Our quarrels dwindled away. Tom showed signs of new energy, left early for work, and looked marvellously well. I felt better, too, but found the opposite about work.

Large doses of sleep had made me invulnerable to worry. From being one of the most conscientious secretaries at the firm of accountants which employed me, always reliable, hard-working and careful, I soon became the laziest and most slapdash. I reasoned with myself as I picked up the phone to report yet another chimerical stomach upset that I had given the firm a year's tense good behaviour and they now owed me some leniency. Besides, it was difficult to sack people these days, and anyway it was nearly Christmas.

I loved the beginning and end of each day. Falling asleep became a swooning pleasure. Sometimes it was like falling slowly down a well, but on other nights it was leaping off the cliff of my pillow into gorgeous spinning blackness. Waking was a warm climb from absolute ease into a state where I lay, half-stunned and splendid, protected for some minutes from the day by the heat-shivering vividness of dreams. The best dream was of the sea, surfy and crystalline, where men raced naked and white as dolphins and I was carried up effortlessly to the point of laughter on great glassy waves.

My new way of life was turning me into an odalisque. I had never before appreciated the pleasures of indolence. I spent hours in the bath, or polishing my fingernails. My face grew sleek and smooth with all this sleep and idleness. At work I was surprised to notice how few people were affected by my new-found langour. One man complained that I was not completing my usual work-load but I merely shrugged my shoulders and made up some story about a broken typewriter. I have shed the load of worry I was born with. I shall never do more for money than I have to again.

One morning just before Christmas, Tom sat with me opening our cards. He was spruce and ready for the office. I was still in my nightdress and had not even combed my hair. We drank tea and slit envelopes with teaspoons. A great batch of cards had arrived, more than a dozen, and soon the coverlet was spread with angels and madonnas and nativity scenes.

'Aren't the stamps pretty this year,' I said, showing Tom the little picture of Joseph with his arm round Mary's shoulder and her hand smoothing the head of the infant Jesus.

Tom's arms held me in a hug.

'You're not too worried about anything much these days, are you?' he commented. He went to the door and stood there, briefcase in hand. 'Lazy girl. I must be off. I'll try not to be late back.'

On Christmas Eve we went to bed early again, and turned to each other. I cannot describe the closeness, the warmth of breath and ideal delight of movement. Ah, he said softly, and fell from me, curved round me, fell soundly asleep with his arms round my neck while I breathed in and out, watching his face in the dusky air. I turned my head and observed my relaxed fingers, the whorls on the palms, the oriental criss-cross patterns on the surface of the skin between the fingers. I saw the early stars, over his head, at the window, and felt I was almost near to understanding about them. I fell asleep.

Flares of gold disturbed the dreamlessness. I became aware of the sun on my eyelids. My eyelashes fringed a private pavilion of hot pale colour. Beneath my cheek the warmth of the pillow was delicious, and I moved my face slightly once or twice to receive the full vellum softness of the linen.

When I opened my eyes, I saw his face asleep on the pillow beside me, one hand cupped under it, fine and serious. Each feature was fine, attenuated, carven, the eyelids solemn and the mouth curved and cut like a fruit. It was cold outside, I could feel the snap of frost in the air on my face, and there was a distant clamour of bells from St Christopher's two roads away. We were warm under our covers.

It was Christmas morning, of course, I thought, taking this as an explanation for the ecstatic complacence which filled me. I leaned across and kissed his curving mouth awake.

What Are Neighbours For

Mrs Brumfitt crossed the room sideways and at speed, making for the comparative obscurity of the corner chair. She was tree-limbed, with beetling unplucked eyebrows that gave her a false scowl. Hilary thanked her for the Mr Kipling Almond Slices, and they talked for a minute or two about *The Jungle Book*, which neither of them had read though Mrs Brumfitt had seen the film. And Mowgli? asked Hilary: any news of Mowgli? Mrs Brumfitt's eyes dimmed to pebbles and she shook her head roughly.

Chitra arrived next and understood at once.

'Ah, poor Mowgli,' she sighed. 'It is the fur coat gang, I saw it on television.'

'You look nice,' said Mrs Brumfitt enviously, wiping her eyes, angry again that her own clean crimplene was the best Large Lady mail order could manage for under fifty pounds.

'Terribly pretty,' agreed Hilary. Her own jeans and

sweatshirt appeared churlish now that she saw they had both made an effort. The lilac of Chitra's shot-silk sari caused her skin to glimmer like verdigris. In her left nostril was a star-shaped diamond, and big silver filigree bells hung from her ears. Her feet peeped out in crimson beaded slippers.

'Here are some cakes from my husband's favourite shop,' she said, 'and here are some pakora which I made myself.'

She arranged herself on the sofa, beaming around her with appreciative delicacy.

'What a lovely room,' she said.

You must be joking, thought Hilary, who had hated this dreary back parlour from the very first day. She unpacked the cakes, which were pistachio green, amber and cream-coloured globes and bars.

'They are made with milk curds that take twelve hours to cook,' called Chitra from the sofa.

'Twelve hours!' said Mrs Brumfitt. 'Some people must have time on their hands.'

Hilary wondered what to do with the pakora, placing them at last between the egg sandwiches and the Scotch pancakes. When she went to open the door for her last guest, Chitra and Mrs Brumfitt were muttering together with some vehemence about their husbands. Only yesterday she had spied Mr Brumfitt from the bathroom window, perched up a ladder fixing a new plastic downpipe while his wife yelled at him, 'You poxy old devil.' Or perhaps it had been, 'You foxy old devil.' Mrs Brumfitt was deeply dissatisfied with him, for the way he refused to eat spiced foods or go out and about or paint the house. When Hilary had asked her to tea, she had responded with immediate wrath: '*I* can't invite anyone round till *he's* decorated.'

Stefania stood puffing in splendour after her climb to Hilary's upstairs maisonette. She was bearing a large pannetone in a sky-blue box.

'For you,' she said, with a grand gesture as though they were both on stage. Her aquamarine dress and della Robbia eyelids dazzled Hilary, who had only seen her before in shapeless coats, generally with a bag on wheels in tow.

'And who else, I wonder, will be here at your tea party?' said Stefania as they walked along the hall. The smile slid from her face like an omelette from its pan when she caught sight of Mrs Brumfitt in the corner. She turned stonily, rearranged her features into some fresh approximation of sweetness, and greeted Chitra with a lordly smile.

'I almost did not come, Hilary,' she said, sinking into a chair. 'I have had *such* a headache all the morning. I said to my husband, this is too much to bear, perhaps I will not go.'

'I hope you feel better now,' said Chitra.

Stefania smiled bravely through half-closed lids, and pressed her temples with her index fingers.

'What about a paracetamol,' said Hilary.

'That's a doctor speaking,' said Mrs Brumfitt.

Stefania shook her head and closed her eyes completely.

'Give me two minutes only,' she whispered.

Hilary thought, if you turned up in my surgery with an act like that, I'd give you short shrift. She was practical and careful in her approach to her work, but a shade

57

underpowered on the empathising front; she took some satisfaction in sending moaning minnies away with fleas in their ears.

'How brave and clever you are to be a doctor,' said Chitra, once they were sitting in a circle around the tea table. 'All that blood.'

'Girls today,' said Mrs Brumfitt. 'There's no stopping them. My Jill, the one who's in computers – you met her, Chitra – well, she makes all her own loose covers and curtains, plays squash, goes to Spanish conversation *and* cooks Rob a hot meal every night.'

'How does she have time for preparing hot meals after work?' asked Chitra.

'She does it all beforehand in a Slow Hotpot,' said Mrs Brumfitt triumphantly, 'then she bungs some baked potatoes in the microwave. That girl is so organised it makes my head spin. She's made time for everything except babies.'

Hilary passed the sandwiches round. She was twenty-nine and had been qualified for two years. She had just managed to land a partnership in a local practice, starting in three weeks' time, after lengthy stints of locum work. Now it looked as though things were about to grind to a close with Philip, more from apathy than for any dramatic reason, plus the fact that he seemed incapable of behaving like an adult. Well, she would be earning enough to be able to buy him out. The question was, whether she should see if she couldn't get pregnant before he left, without telling him, of course. Caroline had managed it before Archie went, and claimed the child was infinitely preferable to the man. This new job gave fairly decent maternity leave, too. She wouldn't be able to afford a nanny yet but she'd have quite enough to pay child-minders, although they'd obviously need to be backed up by a dependable neighbour or two. She looked thoughtfully around the table.

The conversation had turned to animals.

'You know Mowgli has disappeared,' said Chitra to Stefania.

'It was a fox,' said Stefania firmly. 'My Sammy came back four nights ago with deep tooth marks each side of his muzzle. You're not telling me a dog did that.'

'Poor Mrs Brumfitt,' said Chitra softly, watching her next-door neighbour sag in her chair. They had been on friendly terms for a decade now, but Mrs Brumfitt remained on surname terms with everyone and had done so ever since she got married, blighted as she had been with an unmentionable Christian name. Fanny? Boadicea? Whatever it was, nobody was likely to find out. Even her children did not know it. She gnawed savagely at a Grantham gingerbread, fighting back the tears. What that cat had meant to her was nobody's business. Now all she had left to think about was her growth, maybe benign, King's had said, and maybe not. Nobody knew about it except the hospital. It might have been some relief to ask Hilary, her being a doctor, though she probably didn't know much since she was only just out of medical school. Also, she never seemed to have much time for you – she was always in such a tearing hurry – *very* like Jill. This tea was a turn-up for the books. She must be bored waiting for her new job. Either that, or she was after something.

Chitra said, 'In my former life I had cats, dogs, geese,

goats, parrots, so it was a full day running around playing with them all.'

'Spiders are the only one of God's creatures I cannot love,' declared Stefania with an elaborate shudder. 'My God, there was one the size of this teacup on the kitchen floor when I came down this morning.'

'What did you do?' asked Mrs Brumfitt.

Stefania ignored her. Mrs Brumfitt's forehead flushed livid. Chitra became as agitated as a bird.

'Snakes make me full of horror,' she twittered, her eyes large and bright.

'I'm not too keen on eels,' said Hilary.

'Eels!' said Stefania in low thrilling tones. 'I *love* eels! From Condon's I ordered two live eels last February and I carried them home wrapped up in newspaper.'

'Didn't they struggle?' said Hilary.

'No. There is something about being rolled in the newspaper that transfixes them. When I was a young girl in Palinuro, we used to get up in the middle of the night and go down to the stream with forks. Then we stabbed the eels as they swam. How beautiful they were to fry.'

'I like them jellied,' mumbled Mrs Brumfitt, determined to stay in the conversation.

'How delightful, Hilary – chocolate éclairs,' said Stefania, artificial as a West End farce.

'Marks and Sparks,' said Hilary brusquely. She poured more tea.

'I have been reading a book on etiquette,' announced Chitra, 'and it says to add the milk afterwards.'

'*You* put *hot* milk in tea, Chitra, don't you,' said Mrs Brumfitt with interest.

'Oh yes, my first husband always insisted on hot milk,'

said Chitra, and sighed. 'He was a banker. We were used to an enormous social circle. We knew a thousand people. I have gone steadily down. We moved; we knew then maybe five hundred. We moved again. A hundred. Then fifty. Now barely twenty. I have come from the heights in my own country to nothing here in Herne Hill.'

'Herne Hill,' spat Stefania. 'My God, sometime I stand at my front gate and stare at the view of all these red bricks, I think, my *God* how came I into Herne Hill, I who used to look from my front door out over the blue sea.'

'After the war, wasn't it,' commented Mrs Brumfitt. 'No work down your part of Italy.'

Stefania's features writhed.

'How long have you lived here?' asked Hilary hastily.

'Thirty-eight years,' said Stefania, composing herself with an effort.

'Ever since I got married to *him*,' said Mrs Brumfitt, jerking her chin in the direction of her own house.

'How nice it must have been when you both had young children,' said Chitra daringly. 'Did they play together in your gardens?'

'A fair bit,' said Mrs Brumfitt, 'Though Heather and Maria-Grazia used to fight something shocking. I had to throw a bucket of water over them once.'

'Small babies are best,' beamed Chitra. 'All day you can pick them up, put them down, wash them, put them down, clean them up, put them down. But toddlers! Great heavens! Always running here and there! What you must do is get a big strong playpen.'

'I have seven children,' announced Stefania. 'In Italy we love our bambini.'

'Babimbi?' repeated Chitra, tasting the word.

Stefania discharged a cackle of hard-boiled merriment. 'Babimbi, babimbi, babimbi,' she mimicked. Then, as though to an idiot, she leaned across to Chitra and enunciated, 'Bam-been-ee!' She rolled her eyes at Hilary, sharing the joke with someone Educated.

'I do not know Italian,' murmured Chitra, who had, however, a full command of Urdu, Punjabi and Parsee.

'Seven children is a lot,' said Hilary, rather coldly.

'Yes,' shrugged Stefania. 'They came easily. Like rabbits.'

'You love your . . . bambini,' suggested Chitra, polite to the bitter end.

'Of course,' said Stefania. 'I am a good mather. A *very* good mather. They are my life and joy.'

Mrs Brumfitt crumbled the remains of a flapjack between strong nicotine-ochred fingers. Stefania knew that she knew that Stefania had not spoken to her married daughter Paola for two years, even though she was only down the road in Crystal Palace and had a six-month-old baby to cope with. Stefania had not even set eyes on this her first grandchild, and all because of a quarrel which had shot up like a beanstalk from a Boxing Day squabble concerning Darwin's ideas about monkeys. There was also Valerio, with his off-the-back-of-a-lorry dealings and his dodgy nocturnal hours, while Lorella's boohooing, clearly audible through the party wall, regularly kept her awake at night. And Maria-Grazia had gone *right* off the rails. Mrs Brumfitt clamped her mouth shut. This was the umpteenth time over the years that Stefania had decided she wasn't speaking to her for some daft reason or other. Well, she wasn't going to eat dirt again, today or any other day.

'It is a good party, Hilary,' said Chitra, nodding her head and smiling. 'How nice it is to sit here talking about such things with friends. In my country I talk only with the men; I cannot put up with more than twenty minutes with the women because always they talk of the same things: clothes and jewellery, clothes and jewellery.'

'Well, they've got nothing else, have they,' commented Mrs Brumfitt.

'Myself, I like art and the creative life,' Chitra continued. 'I have written poetry, in other places where there was society. Most of it I wrote in Urdu. One only has been English – I wrote about how I was happy to be here but I did not like to see the sad old people stuffed away in Homes.'

It's a toss-up between her and Mrs Brumfitt, thought Hilary. Stefania is obviously a *complete* nightmare.

'Last year I went to pottery classes,' continued Chitra. 'We made beautiful ducks to hang on the wall.' She petered out, dispirited by their lack of interest.

Silence descended over the tea table. Stefania had retreated beneath half-closed azure canopies, brooding on some private bitterness, not bothering to conceal the fact that she was not listening. Mrs Brumfitt was concentrating on the stabbing pains which had started up two or three minutes ago. Were they simple indigestion, or to do with you-know-what?

Hilary felt restless and wondered when she could decently start winding up proceedings. A tea party was the only feasible way she could have got them together without their husbands, but she found all this bread and cake rather disgusting, nothing but refined sugar and carbohydrate. These three looked as though they could do with losing a few stone between them. In fact most of the people she saw wandering around this part of London looked acutely in need of some brisk exercise, as she told them in no uncertain terms when they turned up at her surgery. Out shopping for the cakes that morning she had shaken her head over the sign in the dentist's high street window: 'Free McDonald's voucher with every check-up.'

'I must go now,' said Stefania without warning, waking from her reverie.

'If you must,' said Hilary, who had already mentally dismissed her anyway. She showed her to the door.

Mrs Brumfitt was telling Chitra about her last Sunday outing to Jill's in Lewisham.

'We had a ploughman's lunch in a pub, a piece of cheese *this* size' – folding her napkin into a large triangle – 'stacks of bread, pickle, I don't know how much else, and all for two pounds fifty.'

Hilary looked assessingly at Mrs Brumfitt's mulberry cheeks and meaty forearms; she considered her heavy way of walking, and the coughing sessions she could hear every morning through the kitchen wall as she worked through her bowl of muesli. No, she decided, not without regret; Mrs Brumfitt wouldn't be up to the demands of a young baby for more than an hour at a time, though it might be possible to leave it with her during trips to Safeways or while out jogging. Chitra, on the other hand, looked fit and energetic for her age, and would probably be quite grateful for something like this to help fill her days.

Chitra was fiddling with a bangle, smiling, trying to keep at bay the thought that next month her husband's overbearing, critical and diabetic mother was coming to live with them. The old woman did not speak English and would doubtless do all she could to keep Chitra in the house all day long. She would criticise her to her husband and enlist his support in everything. When she fell ill, she would expect to be nursed as tenderly as a baby. And she would force Chitra to give up her local friendships, dismissing good, kind Mrs Brumfitt as uncouth and this unmarried doctor girl as immoral.

'Those pakora really were super,' said Hilary, in an unaccustomed attempt at ingratiation. 'I'd love the recipe.'

Chitra fluttered her hands.

'They are very easy, but you must have time and patience,' she said. 'One day before your new job begins you must come to my house and watch me make them.'

'You should see her do nan bread,' Mrs Brumfitt chimed in, smacking her lips. 'All puffed up and blistered under the grill.'

'Yes, nan bread too!' said Chitra. 'And also stuffed paratha! We will have another tea party.'

'Just so long as you don't ask the Perfect Mother,' said Mrs Brumfitt. 'Her and her precious bambini. Did you ever? I see nobody's touched those almond slices. Well, I'm not too proud to eat shop-bought. Pass them over, Hilary. By the way, I've been meaning to ask you a favour, I've got something funny here on my side and I was wondering if you'd take a look at it for me one day when you've got a spare minute.'

'Of course,' said Hilary crossly, thinking: honestly! give them an inch.

An Interesting Condition

'Think of your cervix as the sleeve of a sweater,' said the snake-hipped young midwife. Beside her on a beanbag crouched the Health Visitor, knitting away at what looked like a circular bag in meat-pink wool.

No, thought Alice, I won't, and allowed her mind to cast itself back into last night's dream when the new-raised brown beads on her nipples had resolved themselves into fruit seeds, like the gold flecks on strawberries, before easing away to leave her as smooth and pale as before.

Career Girl wrote, 'Cervix = sweater sleeve (?)' in her notebook. Home Birth rearranged her heels on her thighs. Teenager yawned and wriggled. There were nine women in the room, variously disposed at floor level on foam wedges and cushions. Chairs were not part of the Health Centre's Antenatal Class equipment. The women were supposed to seat themselves in such a way as to encourage the stretching of their sacro-iliac joints.

'All those years of Mummy telling me to sit with my legs neatly arranged,' Miss Bandbox had commented. 'And now they tell us to sprawl splayed out all anyhow. She'd have a fit.'

'If your waters break and they are brown, khaki or green,' read the midwife from her clipboard, 'then ring the hospital. The baby's in distress.' Alice stared round the walls for distraction. Professionally printed posters about heroin, Aids, alcoholism and syringe exchanges gave a silly look to the home-made felt-tipped drawings captioned *'Is it Time?'* (a stick woman in a triangular skirt with a pool of water between her feet) and *'How will I Cope?'* (the same stick woman minus her skirt, encircled with syringes and scissors, pear-shaped tears dripping from her face).

'Bruno,' thought Alice, 'Guy, Leonie, Felix, Rosanna, Adrian.' It was Derby Day and she had made Eddie promise that morning to put a pound on the horse of her choice, on his way to work. Her favourite from the list of names was Woodpecker Zeus. Trust you, said Eddie; 300–1. I don't care, said Alice; he sounds lucky.

The midwife drew a plastic-headed rag doll from the jaws of her black bag. A crimson silk sachet was attached to its body by a long cherry-coloured ribbon.

'This is the placenta,' said the midwife, holding up the sachet. 'Have you got the pelvis, Audrey?' The health visitor scrabbled in her carrier bag of wool and produced a large bony structure.

'Excuse me for knitting,' she addressed them chattily. 'I'd hoped to get it finished last night but my husband threw a wobbly. What a shame, it would have made it all so much clearer.'

'Audrey is knitting a womb,' explained the midwife coldly. 'A uterus. Well, you'll just have to imagine. Anyway, the baby starts off inside the uterus, which is a stretchy bag . . .'

Audrey, grinning, raised her knitting needles to display their dangling burden.

'. . . Then it squeezes out and comes down through the pelvis like *this*. But sometimes it gets stuck – like *this*, or *this* – and sometimes it's upside down which usually means a Caesarean. Once it's out, we tug the umbilical cord' – she pulled on the ribbon – 'and out pops the afterbirth.'

'Be prepared for a lot of blood,' said Audrey, nodding sagely. 'I wasn't, I fainted.'

'Coffee time,' said the midwife.

While they dipped digestive biscuits into their plastic beakers, they watched a video of a woman howling in labour. Alice deliberately blurred her vision so that all she could see was an impressionistic moving landscape of seafood and offal.

'*Surely* it can't be like that all the way through,' whispered Career Girl to Alice. 'These must just be the edited highlights, like cricket after the news.'

Alice saw tears perching on the brims of her eyes. The last time *she* had cried was three months ago when she had finally made Eddie understand that it was too late for her to have an abortion. 'Trust you to miss the sell-by date,' he had said.

'Breast-feeding,' said the midwife, snapping off the video. 'We'll have to run through breast-feeding quickly if we're going to squeeze in some relaxation. Here we go then. a) Breast is better than bottle. b) Careful what you eat when breast-feeding – no red wine, tomatoes, garlic or champagne.'

'Guinness is good, though,' interrupted Audrey. *'Lots of vitamins.'*

'Anybody can breast-feed,' said the midwife severely. 'Those who say they can't are only making excuses. Another thing, the baby doesn't suck the breast, it *pumps* it by chomping away with its gums. Its stools should be yellow and watery and not foul-smelling. Sometimes one of your milk ducts gets blocked and that causes mastitis. See a doctor. You might get an abcess too in which case they treat it surgically to let out the pus. Any questions before I move on to the vexed question of cord care?'

'I'd just like to say,' said the fat weary-faced woman seated by the window, 'I'd just like to say that it's not as easy as it looks. I *have* been through it, you see.'

She looked pointedly at the midwife, who obviously had not.

'And what I think,' continued the woman, 'what I think is, bottle-feeding is better. My first was latched on twenty-four hours a day for the first two months. I still wasn't up or dressed by mid-afternoon. Also, it was excruciating. It made me *bleed*. He just sucked on the end like it was a straw. It felt like red-hot pincers. Another thing they don't tell you' – she raked the class with an indignant glare – 'another thing is that milk spurts out in fountains during you-know-what. It's very embarrassing.'

'You've obviously had an unfortunate experience,' interrupted the midwife frigidly. 'Shall we move on?'

'I tried one of those electric breast pumps,' continued the woman inexorably. 'Never do that. I saw my nipple stretching out to six times its length before I could turn the damn thing off.'

'Thank you,' said the midwife, to a general intake of breath and flinching. 'Any questions?'

'Do the brown bumps on your nipples go away?' asked Alice, blushing.

'They're perfectly natural,' said the midwife. 'They're Montgomery's Tubercles.'

'What, as in the Desert Rats?' said Career Girl, looking puzzled.

'They don't ever really disappear,' said the midwife, ignoring her. 'Nor will your breasts be the same. They'll be smaller and less firm than before and they'll have lost their upper roundness. Sometimes after two or three years they start getting back to normal.'

'But by then you'll probably be in the family way again!' interposed Audrey, nodding and smiling.

Mariana, Julian, Victor, thought Alice; Josephine, Basil, Paul. Woodpecker Zeus.

Towards the end of the session, the midwife invited the members of her class to express their feelings about the state of pregnancy, which was perhaps unwise of her.

'It's pretty awful, isn't it?' pleaded Miss Bandbox with a worried laugh. 'I mean, I feel really hideous with all this extra weight and suddenly a double chin and now swollen ankles too.' The class assessed her chin and ankles in silence. She was the dressiest woman there, wearing a scarlet leisure suit appliquéd with characters from Tintin, snow-white socks and navy-blue deck shoes.

'I mean, I don't blame the poor guy for feeling a bit

71

put off,' she continued, smiling desperately. 'What a huge great barrage balloon, what an *elephant*!'

'Body image, body image,' said the midwife abstractedly, identifying the issue and looking up the answer in her notes. 'Be positive. Your newly changing body is not ugly, only different. C.f. slimming, anorexia.'

'Also I can't stand the thought of the actual event,' continued Miss Bandbox. 'It's so undignified, feet in stirrups and all that. I've seriously thought of taking in a mask. Would anyone object, d'you think?'

'What, a *surgical* mask?' asked the midwife.

'No, papier mâché, in the shape of an autumn leaf. I bought it last year in Venice. Then I wouldn't feel so embarrassed by all the doctors and students, not if they couldn't see my face.'

'I think you'll find embarrassment is the least of your worries once you're actually in labour,' said the midwife drily.

'My husband thinks it's a great idea, ' she babbled, laughing fast, unable to stop now. 'He says he's going to bring a bottle of chilled Prosecco, it'll be like the Carnival.'

'I've been earning my living for fifteen years,' said Career Girl suddenly. 'How do I get used to saying please and thank you all of a sudden? He's started throwing his weight around already and I haven't even stopped work yet.'

'Bastard,' said Home Birth. 'My God, *you're* the one who's going through all this and *he's* going to get a share of the baby, isn't he? There ought to be some way they're made to pay.'

'Child-minders,' said the midwife, riffling through her papers. 'Be positive. Marital counselling.'

They ignored her.

'I miss my mates,' said the Teenager. 'I can't go out like this. They'd laugh at me down the disco.'

'I'm bloody lonely,' said another woman with savagery. 'At least you get some social life working in an office, out for a drink of an evening, a good laugh now and then. But stuck in the flat all day? No thank you! I'm going up the wall, listening to that radio chattering on and on, I hear the news six times a day, can't help it, and all those programmes about lemmings and consumer rights and Mrs Antrobus.'

'I listen to the Archers too,' said Audrey brightly. 'Wouldn't miss it for anything.'

'Isolation,' said the midwife. 'Contact your Health Visitor.'

They all looked at Audrey.

'That's me!' said Audrey, shaking her knitting and smiling enthusiastically.

'Does the man *have* to come in with you?' asked Alice. 'I mean, wouldn't it put him off for good?'

'Rubbish!' yelled Home Birth from across the room. 'It does the selfish bastards good to see what we have to go through. My God, *they're* not the ones writhing in agony, are they? Wham bam, thank you ma'am, that's their attitude unless you rub their noses in it. Every woman should *force* the man to be there.'

'We do encourage the mother to bring her partner or at least a friend,' said the midwife. 'The thing is, there simply aren't enough midwives to go round, not to be there with you all the time, anyway.' She checked her watch with evident relief. 'See you next week, ladies, same time, same place. If you're still here, that is.'

Outside, Alice exchanged wary smiles with Career Girl and Miss Bandbox.

'Wasn't that *awful*,' said Bandbox.

'Time for a coffee?' suggested Career Girl.

They heaved themselves around a table at the nearest sandwich bar.

'I keep dreaming about it,' said Bandbox, whose real name was Julie. 'Last night they gave me a carroty little beast with one leg and stunted arms. When I cried they said, Never mind, you'll learn to love it.'

'Have you bought all the equipment yet?' asked Career Girl, who was called Carol. 'Look at this list my friend gave me: six crotch-fastening envelope-necked vests, six babygros, three dozen elasticated disposable nappies, Moses basket for first six weeks, drop-sided cot for afterwards, it goes on and on, I mean, I ask you.'

'You don't have to buy all that,' said Alice stoutly. 'My mother put me in the bottom drawer of her chest-of-drawers when I was a baby. My cousin's just had twins, and *she* sleeps them side by side in an opened-out suitcase.'

'I get back to the house in the evening,' said Carol. 'I go to its room and look at all the silly plastic toys and changing mats that people have already given us, and I think, Why on *earth?* I mean, it's a gigantic red herring, isn't it. That's all it is.'

'What I dread,' drawled Julie in distress, 'what I dread is one of those, you know, those episiotomies. They use *scissors*, you know.'

'What's an episiotomy?' asked Alice.

Julie told her.

'Apparently,' said Carol confidentially, 'the stitches are agony afterwards. You have to sit on a rubber ring for *weeks*.'

'My sister used a packet of frozen peas as a compress because they're, you know, flexible,' said Julie.

'I have heard,' said Carol carefully, tearing the edge of a sugar packet into a frill, 'I have heard that you should freeze a rubber glove full of water and then use the ice fingers one by one as they melt, along the, the affected area.'

'*No!*' squealed Julie.

'I haven't got a freezer,' said Alice.

'And as to the stitches,' continued Carol with relish, 'my sister's friend got a very tired junior doctor in the middle of the night and he stitched her up all along, I mean, the *whole way*, by mistake.'

'*No!*' shrieked Julie.

'Yes,' said Carol. 'They sued. But how embarrassing.'

Alice felt out of it. She was a good six or seven years younger than either of them and none of her friends intended to have babies for years and years. Neither had she, of course.

'My husband's uncle is a gynaecologist,' said Julie. 'He also grows wonderful tomato plants. And can you guess what he puts around their roots?'

They leant forward avidly. She turned pink.

'Placentas!' she whispered.

'No!' said Alice.

'I don't believe it,' said Carol.

'Oh, yes,' said Julie earnestly. 'They're very much in demand, you know, among the hospital staff. Generally the midwives snaffle them because they can sell them to face cream companies for hundreds of pounds. I've told Markie, that's my husband, to insist on having it packed up to take away. I don't see why *I* should subsidise the NHS.'

When she got back to the flat, Alice found the landlady in the hall examining a parcel addressed to her.

'I've just been to the Health Centre's class on how to have a baby,' she volunteered.

'What a waste of taxpayer's money,' snorted old Mrs Ruddle. 'As long as you're well and they can hear the babby's heart beat, forget the rest of it. I had all my four in that same back bedroom where you sleep now. Same bed, too, come to think of it. We used to get married before having babbies in them days,' she added meaningfully.

'We're getting married in February,' said Alice.

'I'll believe it when I see it,' said Mrs Ruddle. 'It's not everyone would have allowed you to stay on. I must be soft.' She stumped off down the hall to her kitchen.

Alice climbed the stairs and crawled straight into the unmade bed. The parcel was from her mother, a book entitled *Wedding Etiquette*, and a note in which she was instructed to Be Nice to Eddie, and, Not to Let Herself Go (More than Necessary).

'Be nice to Eddie,' she said aloud.

A few months ago she had been positively entranced by him. The excitement of moving in together had been acute. But this pregnant state made her feel light years away, as though she were living with an old flame from another decade. She had been kidnapped by lassitude, was grown brutally indifferent to the outside world, and all thoughts had narrowed to the area around her navel.

Even when it emerged that evening, watching the *News at Ten*, that Woodpecker Zeus had romped home while Eddie had failed to place the bet, even then her disappointment at losing chimerical Moses baskets and envelope-necked vests failed to rise to any respectable level of emotion.

'Things on my mind,' said Eddie with truculence. 'Responsibilities.'

I don't much like you, thought Alice.

'You don't much like me,' she said, dishonestly.

'Don't start,' he replied. 'I'm marrying you, aren't I?'

'Who knows,' said Alice.

Who cares, she thought, as sleep descended on the silent roll call: Roland, Charmian, Nina; Belinda, Gabriel, Lee.

Labour

A Dramatic Story
observing not only the Aristotelian Unity of Time
(taking place within twenty-four hours)
but also the later stricter Unities of Place and Action

Dramatis Personae

WOMAN

1st CHORUS OF MIDWIVES

2nd CHORUS OF MIDWIVES

UTERUS   Before impregnation, a small central
female organ shaped like an inverted pear;
by the end of pregnancy, a large bag of
spiral muscle bundles housing the baby;
otherwise known as the womb

CERVIX   Inch-long passage at the low narrow neck
of the uterus; generally closed

PLACENTA   A liverish circular organ grown solely for
the nurture of the baby inside the uterus

VAGINA   Four-inch tube of muscle leading from
cervix to outside world; among other of its
sobriquets: the birth canal

PERINEUM   Area of muscle fibre and blood vessels
between vagina and rectum

BABY

LUCINA   Goddess of Childbirth

ACT I

Scene *A hospital room, with a discreetly glittering and flashing battery of equipment. On a high bed lies the woman, a metal belt monitor girdling her thirty-nine-inch forty-week globe. Beside the bed is a carpet bag from which spills: a plant spray; a Japanese fan; a large stop-watch; a thermos of ice cubes; a wooden back roller. The midwives are checking the monitor's screen, making entries on the partogram chart at the bottom of the bed. A casette-player by the bed plays Edith Piaf's 'Non, Je Ne Regrette Rien'. The wall clock shows 8 p.m.*

CHORUS
    The baby's heartbeat's strong. Unstrap her now.
    Let's check her notes again. Ah yes. We guessed.
    Another fan of Nature's ancient wisdom,
    Not wanting pain relief nor intervention,

81

No forceps, see, nor oxytocin drips
To speed things up. OK, that's fine by us.
Whether she thinks the same in six hours' time
Need not concern us since that's not our shift.

WOMAN   The last couple of weeks have been
spellbindingly hot and still. I confined myself to the
garden, granted temporary immunity from duty,
sympathy, even normal politeness towards other
people by reason of being impregnably pregnant. The
steady, almost solid, golden air along with the damp
clean smell of my own skin were all I cared about. I
felt powerful, magnificent, and perversely *free*. My
liberator rested too, biding its time, making the
occasional dolphin movement when the sun was
strongest on my belly (unborn nine-month eyes
perceive sunshine on the other side as a warm
geranium-shaded lamplight). Then this afternoon the
weather broke. There was a new agitation in the air.
The neighbourhood cats were slinking around, birds
chirred, the trees shook their tops even though there
was no wind. The air turned grey, a milky blue-grey,
and its temperature dropped suddenly though it was
still thick to breathe. Flies buzzed in the kitchen. Then
came the first casual thunder and I was grinning like a
warrior, suddenly savage and excited. The rain came
in isolated splashy drops at first, then soughed into
the flowerbeds releasing passionate garden smells,
purling down the windows, pattering across limp
green leaves and my own still-warm powdery skin.
    I went inside and finished packing my bags,
swapping my chosen tapes at the last minute,

exchanging Dire Straits for *Carmen*, *Spem in Alium* for Eekamouse. How on earth do you choose music by which to give birth? The National Childbirth Trust recommends whale music, those sweet mournful subaquatic sea lullabies sung by toothless baleen whales. Only the males (and then generally only the hump-backed sort) sing these intricately phrased half-hour songs, and then exclusively during the mating season. But in my current incarnation of flesh, whale music sounded almost *too* much of a creature comfort.

CHORUS
    The baby sucks its thumb and bides its time
    Buoyant inside its water-bottle world
    Of amniotic fluid. But nine months on
    The reckoning arrives. Placenta's tired.
    The food's less good. Time to move on. So long.
    Sometimes the cervix's cork provides a sign,
    A show, to free the geni from his jar.
    Sometimes the waters break, which happened here,
    A rush of straw-pale almond-smelling sap,
    So, high and dry, the baby *must* descend.

WOMAN   When the storm took hold of the afternoon and shook the house until its windows rattled, that was the beginning of the end of our time together. I was sad when I realised that this baby will not be one of the rarities born in a caul, delivered with the unruptured membranes covering its face, because *that* would have meant the impossibility of its death by drowning. Now it has lost its own individual ocean and must take its chance along with the rest of us. Soon afterwards, at groin-level or just above, arrived certain dull central pangs. I ignored them for a few hours, dealt with some bedding plants, trailing lobelia and a batch of yellow-eyed heartsease – easy to do, since these pangs were unalarming through familiarity, the usual monthly dullards. But when they grew uglier, pestering me every five or six minutes and hanging around for a minute at a time, so that I was having to stop and grip the garden trowel and concentrate, then, after a final pot of raspberry-leaf tea*, I came here.

ACT II

The wall clock shows 9 p.m.; from the casette-player comes the Toreador's Song. The woman moves slowly round the room changing positions at intervals, leaning against a wall with forehead on folded forearms, sitting backwards astride a chair, kneeling on all fours, etc.

CHORUS
Carmen *again*. She's keen on opera.
Six centimetres dilatation. Good.
In four more hours perhaps – or even less –
The baby will be set to disembark;
Then, Steady as She Goes, and, Land Ahoy!

* 'The ordinary leaves of the raspberry canes from late spring to full summer should be gathered and used (fresh, if possible). Infuse in boiling water and drink freely with milk and sugar. It also makes a good drink with lemon and sugar. It is well-known as particularly good during the later months of pregnancy.' *Food in England*, Dorothy Hartley.

But now it waits, head down, in its old home
The uterus, that muscled bag of tricks,
Which pulls and squeezes with increasing force
Tugging the cervix up over its head
A little more with every strong contraction
On average one centimetre an hour,
Until there is no length but only width.
(In the same way, Caruso's head was perched
Neckless upon his shoulders – that great voice
A direct product of its shortened passage.)
Eight score contractions for a first-time child
And half that count for each one after that;
Slow work, irksome, and most laborious.

WOMAN Come home with your shield or on it, said
the Spartan mother to her son. When we were
children we used to play dares, stay silent through a
two-minute Chinese burn, grip a stinging nettle and
not cry. I don't know what we thought would come
from this, but something did, some sort of safety. I
knew before I was eleven that I wasn't a scaredy cat
and I still know it. What's about to happen may well
be another less childish sort of mettle detector. Excuse
me for a minute . . .

(Woman falls silent, concentrates on the clock, fetches quick
shallow breaths like a cat in hot weather.)

CHORUS
That's right, relax your jaw and shoulders now;
Keep your eyes open, focus on that clock
And concentrate, still while your body works.
We only shut our eyes for pleasant things,
Kissing, and other stuff that leads to this.

85

WOMAN The approach of labour is unnerving because nobody seems to agree on the *nature* of the pain involved. Susan told me, think of the worst possible pain you can imagine and it's a hundred times worse than that. Her labour lasted twenty-four hours, during the course of which she progressed from deep breaths of laughing gas, which made her dopey but did not take away the pain, to injections of pethidine, which made her sick and vague but did not take away the pain, to an epidural (the plastic tube of numbing liquid inserted through a hollow needle between two vertebrae in your spine), which took away the pain but also removed her capacity to work with her body's pushing urges and so necessitated the baby's forcible forceps removal, which, what with tearing and bruising and stitches both internal and external, meant several more weeks' pain afterwards.

On the other hand, Nicola said that most of her first birth had been no worse than very bad period pains, except at the end, when it felt like an extremely constipated bowel movement involving a coconut.

CHORUS

    This talk of pain relief and active birth's
    All very well, but what they really need
    Are more midwives with more experience.
    We have more patience and more creature feeling
    For our own sex; know to leave well alone,
    Don't crave control or intervene through pride
    Like certain doctors we could mention. No.
    We watch, wait, check, cheer, wait, and give advice.
    Before, we'd see each drama to its close,

Before, that is, shift-work became the rule.
Now, though, our drop-out rate's eighty per cent.
Long training with no money at the end,
This no-strike policy and powerlessness
Do not encourage us to persevere.
Good luck, dear, we're off now to Burgerland.
Here comes the next shift ready to take over.
Remember us. Women should help each other.
And *this*, if nothing else, is women's work.

(Second chorus of midwives enters room, checks charts, exchanges pleasantries, yawns; woman carries on alone, practising her positions and concentrating.)

WOMAN   All the pain so far has been well below the belt and I imagine it will remain that way. So I shall stay upright, whether standing, sitting or kneeling, for as long as I can, right to the end if possible. That way I'll be on top of it. Whenever I've heard contractions described with any attempt at vividness it's always been in melodramatic terms: 'great breakers surging in the black sea of the body,' and so on. I will try to avoid such clichés. Still, to be fair, now I'm actually in the middle of it, I can appreciate the maritime imagery. Contractions *do* come in waves, each building to a crest and leaving a respectable breathing space in between. Otherwise I wouldn't be able to talk to you like this, even if I *am* speaking rather fast.

Last year I had a violent fortnight down on the French south Atlantic, where the coast follows a pencil-straight line for hundreds of kilometres. I have never known bathing like it. It tugged off swimming costumes and teased out mad laughter and screaming.

This sea was not to play with but to play dares against.
Cross-currents and the suction of incoming waves
kept up a continual state of tension only just this side
of pleasure. Sometimes, watching the water rear up a
few yards from you, towering in a curved wall to
block the light, you quailed and forgot to swim into it;
then it would break over your head, sweep you off
down underneath, nose and mouth filled with brine
in a dark, stinging thuddingly silent world.
Sometimes, best of all, you steered into and on top of
a great boiling wave which had not quite broken, and
then you were riding blithely on its crash and roar.
You have to keep your spirits up against that sort of
sea, shout and sing and concentrate hard on
anticipating the violence while holding your body
quiet and prepared.

ACT III

*The clock shows 4 a.m. The woman is sitting restlessly astride
a chair, head on hands on chairback, making an assortment
of noises – muttering, grunting, singing disjointed phrases.*

2nd CHORUS
    She's reached the state which marks transition
    From waiting into thrustful energy.
    Contractions double up and lose their rhythm,
    Heavy to ride, intractable, austere.
    The baby's almost ready – but not quite –
    Must wait until the cervix's front edge

(Otherwise known as the anterior lip)
Withdraws in self-effacement round the skull
At last allowing space for exodus.

WOMAN   What I forgot to take into account about pain
at the start of all this was the way it wears you down
when it goes on and on. I've been at it now for nine
hours. Excuse me.
Mmmmarrh. Mmmmarrh. I'll give you one-O.
Green grown the rushes-O.
When I time a contraction by the second hand of
my watch, I now find it's lasting almost two minutes,
while the rests in between are getting so short that
sometimes there's no breathing space at all. Then just
when I think I'm managing, it turns into something
else so that I'm wrestling with unknown quantities
like the strong man in the myth. It's not fair.
Mmmmarrh. Mmmarrh. What is your one-O?
Mmmarrh. One is one and all alone – lalalalaLA – and
evermore shall be so.
And that's a lie as well. One *isn't* one. One isn't
quite oneself at all today. One is, in fact, almost two.
And ANOTHER. Come on you Spu-urs. Come on
you Spu-urs. You'll nev-er walk alone.

(Shouts colourfully.)

I've had enough of this. It's got beyond a joke. They
told me at the classes to do without pain relief if
possible. 'Better for the mother.' RUBBISH! 'Better for
Baby.' B***** Baby! I should have had that injection
in the spine at the start of all this, the one that
paralyses you from the waist down, the one where

89

you can play scrabble during it. It was all the talk of
scrabble that put me off. Every time the word epidural
was mentioned, scrabble came up too. I hate scrabble.
GIVE ME AN EPIDURAL *NOW*!

2nd CHORUS
Too late, dear, sorry, much too late for *that*.
You're nearly there. An epidural now
Would take too long to work, would slow you
    down.
Nor can we give you pethidine – too late!
It might slow down the baby's breathing speed.
Why don't you try a little laughing gas?

*(They hand her a mask, show her how to put it over her face;
she sucks in deep breaths.)*

They all do this, the nature's-children set,
Leave it too late then yell for pain relief.

(To woman)

Not long now dear. Be patient. Don't push yet.
Try lighter breathing – Hoo Hoo Ha Ha Ha.

WOMAN   Who? Who? Ha! Haha!

ACT IV

*The clock shows 5 a.m. The woman is sitting propped against
pillows, high on the delivery bed, sideways on to the audience.
The midwives stand around her, showing more animation*

90

than they have done up till now. From the casette-player
comes Lone Ranger's 'Push, lady, push', the reggae song
whose chorus runs, 'Push, lady, push, lady, push; Push and
make a youth-man born'.

2nd CHORUS
> Strongly embraced by each contraction
> The baby, hugged and squeezed, waits upside down
> Until the lock's enlarged before it's launched
> Headfirst, chin tucked to chest, in slow motion
> Through vaults of bone, branched pelvic
>   arabesques,
> And down along the elastic boulevards.

WOMAN   Ah, the relief! No more forcible dawdling, no
more long-suffering waiting in the wings! Now I can
get some *work* done.
> Hgnagggh! Hgnagggh!

(Makes other serving-for-match-point noises.)

And here's my whole body working away like a pair
of bellows, sweating with aspiration, intent on
exhaling a brand-new bellowing homunculus.

(Roars.)

See these women staring so avidly between my legs?
These are my trusty accoucheuses who have whiled
away much of this drama's time with hypothetical
knitting, but who now wait, breath bated, for the first
gasp.

(Roars again.)

2nd CHORUS
    The baby's nearly here – we see its head,
    We glimpse the unfused soft-skulled fontanelle.
    Now it draws back again. Stop pushing, dear,
    Or else you might get torn. You don't want *that*.
    Breathe very lightly, puff from West Wind cheeks,
    Hold baby back with candle-flickering breaths.
    Keep your mouth soft and you'll be wide down
        there.

WOMAN   So *that* accounts for all the pouting that goes
    on. I wondered what was behind it. Well, prunes and
    prisms, prunes and prisms, prunes and prisms.

(Takes shallow panting breaths.)

    Gently they receive its head; they lead out each
    shoulder in turn. And now – it – glides – into – the –
    world . . . away from me.

*(The midwives crowd in, obscuring the woman from sight. A
thin infantile wail rises, gathering strength.)*

ACT V

*The wall clock shows 6 a.m. The woman lies on the bed. The
baby is at her breast. The midwives are still grouped round
her lower half, obscuring the view.*

2nd CHORUS
    After the birth must come the afterbirth.

92

A shot of syntometrine in her thigh
Will speed things up. Contractions start again;
We tug the rainbow cord still linking them,
Its two-foot length still beating with their blood,
And out slides the placenta. Animals
Gulp down this liverish morsel routinely –
Its succulence keeps up the mother's strength –
And even among certain human tribes
It's called the midwife's perk. Once in a while
Some earthy type who's read too much insists
We pack it up for her to cook at home.
Not this one. Quite the opposite in fact;
She hasn't even noticed what's gone on.

WOMAN You were storm-blue at first, covered with
white curds of vernix. Next you turned pink like a
piece of litmus paper. They gave you a lick and a
promise, then handed you back to me, your limbs
lashing, your face a mask of anger. I felt like a
shipwreck, but you fell silent, little Caliban, and
latched on. After that spread-eagling storm we were
washed up onto the beach together. Now you're quiet
as a limpet on a piece of driftwood.
  How can I ever think of love again?

*(Midwives still grouped staring between her legs. A hand is
seen, rising and falling, wielding needle and thread.)*

2nd CHORUS
Congratulations, dear. Only one stitch.
You hardly tore at all, you lucky girl.
If Doctor had been here you would need more.
The commonest operation in the West,

Top favourite, is episiotomy,
With one hour's careful stitching afterwards.
They cut the perineum – to make space
For baby's head, they say – unkindest cut
Of all, through muscle layers. Less haste, we say,
Less eagerness to hurry things along,
More willingness to wait, more gentleness,
Would favour women's future love lives more.
Remember, love makes babies after all.

(Enter Lucina, strong, broad-hipped, big-bosomed, carrying a bundle of wheat in one hand and a silver kidney dish in the other.)

LUCINA   As Goddess of Childbirth, it behoves me to point out that such trivial complaints about the possibly diminished quality of her future sex life are light-minded in the extreme. The fact is, *she's* alive and the *baby's* alive. You seem to take that for granted, and yet a hundred years ago – no, even *fifty* years ago – her friends and family would have been sending up heart-felt thanks to me for her safe delivery. It's no tea party, you know, even now, and it's not meant to be. You'll recall how Eve was told, 'In sorrow thou shalt bring forth children,' as the bishops quoted at Queen Victoria when they heard she'd accepted sniffs of the new-fangled anaesthetic chloroform (although *that* didn't stop her using it the next time, and the next). My goodness, women are so *spoilt* these days.

   I even hear them complaining if they have to have a Caesarean. They'd have had a sight more to

94

complain about during *my* heyday, when the Roman
Lex Caesarea forbade the burial of a dead pregnant
woman before the baby had been cut from her womb.
A certain number of babies have always got stuck on
their way out, but at least now you've got forceps and
ventouse suction and other such gadgets to help
things along. Not so long ago they were still having to
hack awkward infants out piecemeal, cutting off
protruding limbs, coaxing out what remained with
pot-hooks, spoons, forks and thatchers' hooks. Many's
the time I've seen one midwife take hold of the
mother and the other seize the emerging baby, both
pulling and tugging for all they're worth. And of
course, with your short memories, you'll have
forgotten puerperal fever? *That* was caused after the
birth of the child by bacteria creeping up through the
still-open cervix and infecting the womb. Women
died raving. Oh yes, puerperal fever killed more
mothers than all the other things put together. So the
woman in this little drama should thank her lucky
stars and Joseph Lister that she's living in an age of
antisepsis. She may well be a bit bruised and stitched
and shocked, but at least she's still here.

I can never get over what a short memory the
human race has. It makes me impatient, it really does.
Why, these days, you hardly know you're *born*.

Christmas Jezebels

A seasonal story dedicated to St Nicholas,
patron saint of (among others) prostitutes

The three sisters lay curled asleep together like cats in a basket. They had always shared this truckle bed; and, as they had grown older and larger, it had become increasingly crowded. There seemed little hope of an improvement in the situation, however, since the family's cash-flow problems were by now quite hair-raising.

Beatrice was the first to wake, frowning and snarling her way out of some dream argument. At eighteen she was the oldest of the sisters, and the most worried. Opposite her snored Isobel, a better pragmatist at sixteen than she would ever be; and in the middle lay her favourite, Jessica, an unnervingly brainy child of twelve.

It was still very early, but already Beatrice could hear the fishermen down on the beach. The uncurtained window showed December stars fading into another fourth-century Lycian morning.

'Time to get up,' she announced at last, throwing off their blanket of patchwork sacking. Not being able to afford nightdresses, they slept in their underwear, though they were fastidious girls and always hung their stockings to dry at the fireplace before going to bed.

'Oh no,' said Beatrice.

'What's the matter?' asked her sisters as they shuffled out of bed.

'He's finally lost his reason,' said Beatrice, staring at the pile of unfamiliar garments on the chair.

'Look at *these*,' said Jessica, holding up a pair of transparent frilly drawers edged with red ribbon.

Isobel sniggered to herself as she buckled on a stiffly-boned satin bra.

'Don't you dare *touch* these filthy rags!' thundered Beatrice.

'Why not?' asked Isobel. 'We can't go round in our pants and vests all day, and he's obviously pawned our usual clothes.' She pranced over to the little mirror and started to wind a feather boa around her neck.

'Such *obvious* garments almost parody his intention,' observed Jessica. 'I suppose he expects *me* to wear this babyishly short smock with the teddy bear appliqués.'

'Oh, my poor lamb,' moaned Beatrice, hugging her sister. 'Little do you realise.'

'I think I do, you know,' said Jessica. 'He wants you two to dress as *filles de joie*, but he's decided to aim me at the paedophile market.'

Isobel had by now wriggled into a leather jerkin and was squeezing her feet into a pair of high fur-rimmed mules.

'It's a disgrace,' said Beatrice, and sat down on the edge of the bed in tears.

'Don't worry, Beet,' called Isobel from the mirror. 'I'm

not going to fall in with his wicked plans. I just like dressing up.'

Jessica put her arm round Beatrice's heaving shoulders.

'You know what he's like when he gets a bee in his bonnet,' she said soothingly.

'But he's serious this time,' sobbed Beatrice. 'And we haven't got any money at all. And he's taken our clo-othes!'

'Well, I'm certainly not going to wear that baby's dress,' said Jessica decisively. 'And you would look as ridiculous in a *guêpière* as he would. So I suggest we tear the bedspread in half and share it. We can cut head holes in the middle, and pull it all together with string belts.'

'Do cheer up,' said Isobel. 'We're going to have to stay cool and present a united front, or we're done for.'

'Meanwhile, I'll send a letter of protest to the Bishop,' said Jessica.

'Oh, well, *that's* all right then,' said Isobel.

Down in the kitchen, they found their father, Mack, looking shifty and making toast.

'Ah, there you are, my dears,' he smiled, avoiding their eyes. 'My goodness, Isobel, don't you look a picture! Quite the glamour girl. But why aren't my other daughters dolled up in their nice new clothes? I went to considerable trouble and expense, you know . . .'

'Oh, cut the cackle, Daddy,' said Isobel. 'We know what you're up to.'

'I think you're absolutely disgusting,' said Beatrice, cutting more bread for their breakfast.

'I can't carry on like this,' said Mack resentfully. 'It's not fair to take that line. I've only got your best interests at heart, and I don't want to see you starve. You're eating me out of house and home. Look at Beatrice wolfing down that last crust. I know you're growing girls, but we're getting through five loaves a week. We've sold everything we can. Nobody will marry you because you haven't got dowries . . .'

'No, you drank them after mother died,' interrupted Beatrice.

'. . . And quite frankly, you're *my* daughters and it's about time you started bringing in some money.'

'Why don't you go out and get a job?' asked Isobel. 'After all, you're a qualified herring-gutter.'

'Times are hard!' he snapped. 'You can't just walk into a job these days.'

'I wish we *could* get jobs and help you, Daddy,' said Jessica. 'But we're not trained to do anything.'

'That's the beauty of what I'm suggesting, my dear!' he beamed at her. 'You don't need qualifications!'

'Aren't you ashamed of trying to force your own daughters into a life of trollopdom?' enquired Beatrice coldly.

'Watch your language!' barked Mack. 'No, no. You've misunderstood. I want you to have *careers*. And the best career opening for any woman just now is as a hostess.'

'A hostess? A streetwalker, you mean,' said Beatrice.

'Who said anything about streets?' he asked tetchily. 'You would be doing business in the comfort of your own home, with all the benefits of a freelance's life. You could break for meals whenever you wanted, and fit the housework in round clients at your own leisure. I can't see any drawbacks myself.'

'There wouldn't *be* any for you, that's why,' said Isobel.

'Except a bad conscience,' added Beatrice.

'Look, there's nothing *wrong* in the job,' said Mack in self-righteous tones. 'It's natural, after all, and it's useful to society. Think of the loneliness and frustration of travellers on their own, or of sailors like that bunch from Tripolis last week. If they're able to pass their time in agreeable company and relieve their natural urges, then they're not going to go round smashing windows and beating up peaceful citizens, are they? It stands to reason.'

'So you mean we'd be like social workers?' asked Jessica.

'Just give it some thought,' snarled Mack. He locked them in the kitchen and shouted 'Back at lunch-time' through the keyhole.

'There always seems to be enough for a glass of retsina,' said Isobel resentfully.

'He's gone to drum up custom,' said Beatrice.

'We've finished the bread and there's nothing for lunch,' said Jessica.

Early in the afternoon, Mack returned to the attack.

'You're lovely girls, all of you,' he said, and on his breath was the fermented smell of loquacity with which they were so familiar. 'Even you, Beatrice. *Big* girl. Nice manners too, most of the time. Oh, we brought you up well.' He dashed moisture from his eye. 'You'll make a good team.'

'I'm worried that our team has only a very limited appeal,' mused Isobel. 'I mean, as an all-girl affair, we're completely missing a large section of the market. Why don't *you* join us as a working partner, Father? You're still a fine figure of a man, and you know what sailors are. Not to mention the boys who come over from Macedonia.'

Mack stared at her sorrowfully from eyes spider-veined with alcohol and sunlight.

'I'm ashamed to hear a daughter of mine talk like that,' he said. 'The trouble with you girls is that you don't know what life is about. The act of love between two people is a very beautiful thing. It's not a subject for snickering over. You're not being asked to do anything unnatural. No more than one at a time.' He paused. 'Even though we'd make a lot more like that,' he added thoughtfully.

'I'm hungry,' said Jessica.

'Blame your sisters, then, and your own pig-headed-ness,' said Mack.

'I'd rather starve to death than do what you're asking,' said Beatrice.

'Oh yes?' said Mack. 'You think life's a big tea party, don't you? You think you were born with a meal ticket. Well, let me tell you, there's no such thing as a free lunch.'

'I never said there was,' said Beatrice. 'But I happen to know what I want from life, which is half the battle.'

'Oh yes?' said Mack again, heavily ironic. 'What's that, then?'

'Freedom, and the same chances as men to earn my living.'

'I want money and pleasure, but only with self-respect,' added Isobel.

'What about you, madam?' asked Mack, glaring at Jessica. 'I suppose you've got it all worked out too?'

'Oh, I want true love, by which I mean a tender and enduring passion based on moral judgment and mutual esteem,' said the girl.

Mack took a spotted handkerchief from his pocket and wearily wiped his forehead.

'We're not *getting* anywhere, are we,' he said sadly at last. 'Let's face it, my dears. Times are hard. Think of the little friends you used to play with down on the seashore. The Okapi girls are all working for *their* father. The Giliki family have virtually cornered the market down by the Goat in Boots, what with their spangled counterpanes and their oyster-scented candles. They probably didn't particularly *want* to do it at first — they'd rather have been lounging around in armchairs all day — but they couldn't make money any other way and they felt a very proper sense of duty towards their loving parents.'

The girls remained silent.

'You can't *do* anything else,' reasoned Mack. 'Well, you could hem togas from five in the morning till midnight for two lire a week, I suppose, but that wouldn't keep us in bread, and it would ruin your poor eyes. If I turned you out of the house to fend for yourselves, you'd each of you be doing what I'm suggesting inside three months, but without my protection or a roof over your heads.'

'And what would *your* cut be, Father?' asked Isobel keenly. 'What percentage would *you* take?'

'Naturally I would have to deduct your board and

lodging, so that would include the mortgage and all bills. But that's not the point. No, it would be a two-way process. I'd find the clients and take away all that unfeminine business of haggling; you would be left free to concentrate on being pleasant and pretty.'

'Oh, Father,' burst out Beatrice, 'What would our mother say if she could hear you now?'

'I won't have you dragging your mother into this,' shouted Mack, his temper in shreds at last, slamming his way out of the kitchen and back to the Goat in Boots without, however, forgetting to lock the door behind him.

The girls passed a long afternoon discussing their predicament. Jessica had noticed on the way downstairs to breakfast that morning that the parlour had been divided by makeshift curtains of sacking and old fishing nets into several small cubicles. This observation now assumed a sinister significance in their minds.

'He's planning a major assault tonight,' commented Isobel. 'So we must take precautions.'

Accordingly they made what preparations they could.

In the early evening Mack put his head round the door and winked at them roguishly.

'I'm throwing an impromptu cocktail party, girlies,' he said. 'But for goodness' sake do something about your faces. You're all as white as turnips. You could at least dab some cochineal on your mouths; it's in the pantry. Hurry up, though. I want you to meet my friends.'

'Let's have a butcher's,' came a voice from somewhere close behind him.

'Not *yet*,' he hissed, and closed the door again.

'Here we go,' said Isobel, and the sisters kissed each other before trooping upstairs to the parlour.

'Let me introduce you to my gorgeous daughters, gentlemen,' said Mack, sweating and smiling like a crocodile. By the window stood three men holding thimblefuls of Mack's best Smyrna liqueur. The girls eyed them up and down with interest.

'Not a pretty sight,' muttered Isobel.

The most self-assured was a heavily built blond of about fifty, expensively dressed, his velvet shoulders lavishly powdered with scurf.

'Beatrice, my dear,' said Mack, 'This is Mr, er . . .'

'No names,' said the man.

'No pack-drill,' responded Beatrice smartly. Mack pinched her and took her to one side.

'He's a very important man, and he's rolling in it,' he hissed. 'Be nice to him or I'll knock your teeth down your throat.'

Isobel had been staring with interest at another of the men, a blushing bull-necked redhead with skin like orange peel.

'Well, if it isn't Mr Soska!' she called gaily across the room. 'He's the police constable from Apamicea, where Aunt Sophia lives,' she added, as if in explanation to Jessica.

'Will you be *quiet*!' hissed Mack, steering her towards a cubicle and throwing a smile which was both appalled and fawning at the policeman, who was by now incapable of raising his eyes from the ground.

'And this is my youngest child, little Jessica,' said Mack

to the remaining customer, a jittery old greybeard with a swinish eye.

'You're quite sure she's, ah, as we discussed?'

'Oh *yes*,' enthused Mack, 'all my girls are guaranteed absolutely intacta, of course, but this one even more so.' He breathed a sigh of relief as he watched the old man lead his youngest daughter away.

Beatrice was explaining her position to the nameless man.

'I'm afraid I can't possibly do what you're suggesting as I live my life by the Kantian Imperative,' she said. 'Do you know it? "Act in such a way that you never treat humanity, either in your own person or in the person of others, as a means only, but always equally as an end."'

'No problem,' he sniggered. 'I want your end for my own means.'

'As far as I can see, mutual desire or generative impulses are the only proper motives for the sexual act,' she said as she dodged his grip. 'But you are trying to use my poverty to buy me. Doesn't it make you weep to see how vast numbers of people are forced by the wolf at the door to sell themselves to the wolf in the bed?'

'Don't give me that,' he snarled, grappling with the string around her sacking robe. 'Girls go on the game because they enjoy it.'

'So you think the real attractions for me are your surface moistness as of a cheese in summer and the way spit crowds the corners of your dewlaps,' panted Beatrice.

'Just shut up and lie down! I don't pay you to talk.'

'For your own sake I think you should buy a blow-up rubber doll,' she gasped, parrying a clumsy rabbit punch with ease. 'Because you're harming yourself even more than me by taking that attitude towards a fellow member of the human race.'

They wrestled each other into a swaying clinch.

'I can see your dilemma, I can really, and I sympathise,' she continued. 'Even so, I haven't yet mastered the art of transcendental meditation and I can't divorce my body from the rest of me while you use it to give yourself relief.'

By this time the man had inched and grappled her over towards the bed, and now he tipped her onto it. Holding her down with his knee, he paused to unbutton himself, but when he looked up she had produced a large carving knife from inside her dress.

'Go away,' she said, and her new terseness of speech must have affected him more powerfully than her eloquence, for he did as he was told.

Meanwhile, Isobel was having an altogether homelier conversation with the policeman.

'And how's your wife's cystitis?' she asked chattily. 'If it *was* cystitis. You never know what you might catch these days. And the children? Let's see, five of each, aren't there?'

The policeman nodded miserably. One of his hands shot out as if of its own volition and fastened itself to Isobel's left breast. She detached it and put it back in his lap.

'What's the matter?' she asked sweetly. 'Doesn't your wife understand you?'

'She's got ten kids,' said the policeman at last. '*You're* the one that doesn't understand me.'

'Why not try explaining?'

'It's the facts of life, isn't it. I've always got on well with girls like you. I don't give them too much trouble.

107

What I say is, girls like you are vital to society.'

'How do you mean? And I *wish* you wouldn't do that.'

'Sorry. Well, you know what they say. "Sewers are necessary to guarantee the wholesomeness of palaces." The palaces being lawful marriages, you see,' he added helpfully.

'*I* see,' said Isobel thoughtfully. 'I must say, I've never heard *that* used as a chat-up line before.'

'How about it, then?' he asked.

'Sorry,' said Isobel. 'I've got a headache.'

'Funny. I don't feel much like it myself now,' he said glumly.

In the third cubicle, Jessica was finding it difficult to stay polite towards the old man.

'You're a nice little girl, aren't you!' he said with enthusiasm, pinching her cheek.

'Thank you,' she answered coldly.

'And what do you want to do when you grow up to be a big lady?' He brushed his knuckles across her chest with avuncular jocularity. 'Although that's a long way off, I can tell.'

'I want to be an astrologer,' said Jessica, pulling away. 'And I'm also tempted by certain aspects of moral philosophy.'

'My goodness. Is that so,' he said, temporarily slowed down.

'It is. I can't help agreeing with Aristotle who, when questioned as to what could possibly make this life worth living, answered, "For the sake of viewing the heavens and the whole order of the universe."'

'My, my. All those long words. You mustn't tire yourself.' He tugged her over to the couch and pulled her onto his knee. 'Why don't you have a little sleep,' he suggested in an abstracted manner, and his hands began moving with expert energy over her thin body. At this point, Jessica remembered her sisters' words and, wriggling from his lap, she kicked him as hard as she could exactly where they had told her.

Mack's fury was terrible to see.

'Now you've really gone and done it!' he yelled. 'They'll tell everybody you're no good! I could kill you!'

He picked up the poker and made a run at Isobel, but Beatrice felled him with the kitchen chair.

While he lay moaning, momentarily stunned, the sisters ran upstairs and barricaded themselves inside their bedroom.

'He'll have cooled down by tomorrow,' said Isobel, without much conviction.

'We're going to starve,' said Beatrice, who was by now extremely hungry.

'Let's go to bed,' suggested Jessica. 'Things always look better in the morning.'

'What *happens* to people as they get older?' mused Isobel as she brushed her hair.

'Try not to think about it,' shuddered Beatrice.

They fell asleep to the rhythmic sussuration of the sea.

It was still very early but already there were shoals of fishermen down on the beach. The uncurtained window showed the December stars fading into yet another Lycian morning.

All three girls were woken at the same moment by a violent racket from the chimney-breast.

'It's Father!' screamed Beatrice. 'He's climbed down from the roof and he's going to kill us!'

'Don't be stupid,' said Isobel. 'Some of the bricks must have come loose. Wait till the soot clears.'

But Jessica had hopped out of bed to investigate.

'Happy Christmas from Nicholas, Bishop of Myra,' she read aloud from the festive card she found in the grate. Then she discovered that their stockings, which they had hung up to dry as usual the night before, were bulging with gold pieces.

'Your letter to the Bishop!' breathed Isobel, smiling and running her fingers through the gold.

'We're saved!' crowed Beatrice. 'The man's a saint!'

Mack, his forehead embellished with a bump the size of a seagull's egg, stared stupidly at the bullion.

'It's mine, of course,' he said tentatively. 'I mean, you're my daughters, so that's obvious.' He noticed the expressions on their faces and began to backpedal speedily. 'But I'll put most of it towards your dowries,' he said. 'The lads down at the Goat in Boots *will* be pleased to know you're up for grabs again. Any number of them have said they'd marry you if you only had dowries.'

'Actually, Father,' said Beatrice carefully, 'I'd rather put my money into property. I think it's a better invest-ment. I thought I'd set up a bed and breakfast down by the harbour, a nice orderly house with lights out at eleven and grilled herrings at eight.'

'Don't you *want* to get married?' asked Mack, appalled.

110

'To be quite honest, I've gone off the idea for some reason.'

'I was reading somewhere the other day', said Jessica, 'that marriage is only a legalised version of what you had planned for us anyway.'

'You really are a nasty-minded little brat, aren't you,' said Mack.

'Don't say so, Daddy!' she cried, her eyes filling. 'I want to make sure you're all right. I'm going to stay for a while and teach you how to cook and wash for yourself.'

'And then?' snarled Mack.

'Then I'm going to live with Beatrice. She says I can have a big room with a balcony overlooking the sea. There should be an excellent view of the heavens. I shall buy the biggest, most powerful telescope in the world.'

'Steady *on*,' murmured Isobel.

'I suppose you're off too, then,' said Mack, rounding on her.

'Correct,' she said. 'I've always wanted to travel. I've got a boyfriend my own age you don't know about. He hasn't got any money. We've been pipe-dreaming about moving to Persepolis to manage a dance troupe. Now we'll be able to do it.'

'You're going abroad with some boy on your *own?*' asked Mack, scandalised. 'I suppose you realise no one will ever marry you if you do that, you stupid strumpet?'

'Listen, Father, I hope I will never be driven to what you were suggesting last night,' she said severely. 'And now that I've got money, you surely don't think I'm going to allow a pack of greedy hypocritical men like yourself to lay down the law to me about love?'

'Bravo!' cried Beatrice, hugging her sister.

'Bravo!' carolled Jessica, dancing off round the room. 'Yuletide blessings on us all! And our most cordial compliments of the season to the good Bishop!'

A Shining Example

The two women faced each other across the garden table like rival queens from a pack of playing cards. Mrs Leversage obviously ruled the clubs and spades, with her coal-coloured hair catching rookish blue lights from the sun.

'So that was why I left Fowler and Crabpiece,' she concluded. 'The job was simply not creative or fulfilling enough to warrant my staying. You, Jane, of all my friends, would understand that.'

Jane looked down at her lap in gratification at being so included into the blessed company of Mrs Leversage's friends. Here was a most unassuming queen of hearts and diamonds. The only rage-red item which qualified this girl for such a title was her hair, which crackled in a silent blaze around her white cheeks and forehead.

'What exactly did you do at Fowler and Crabpiece?' she asked in a respectful voice.

'A great deal of liaison work and coordination,'

snapped Mrs Leversage. 'It's difficult to describe, but, my God, they certainly squeezed every ounce they could from me. Some nights I was there until seven o'clock. It was *exhausting*. But I wouldn't have minded any of that if there had only been more frankness and less jealousy flying around. Certain people simply closed their eyes and refused to recognise my talents. When that happens, it's time to leave.'

'Do you mean, you wish you could have been more *in charge* of things?'

'Well, naturally responsibility arrives hand in hand with recognition of one's talent and value to the company as a whole. But that's not really the point. I don't think you've quite grasped the issue, Jane.'

'I'm sorry. I've never had that sort of job. I don't really think about my work except as work. It's just something I have to do for the money and I'm glad when Friday comes. But of course your work isn't really *work*.' She struggled wrinkling with effort, hurrying on as she saw Mrs Leversage's face shift into opaque displeasure. 'I mean, you don't need the money. You're doing it for another reason altogether. A *creative* reason!'

Mrs Leversage shifted in her chair and searched the girl's face for satire. She saw nothing but a desire to please. The mention of money had touched her on the raw. Only last night her husband had been twitting her about the expense of the working wardrobe which she had purchased before starting at Fowler and Crabpiece; she had not stayed long enough to recoup even half its cost from her salary.

'Your mind is too full of money,' she said. 'There are other things in life.'

'Sorry,' muttered Jane. She fiddled with the glass ring she was wearing, twisting it so that its refracted lights fell in a shower of arrows onto the darkness of the bay tree by their table.

'What on *earth* are you wearing on your finger?'

'Only my diamond ring,' said Jane, with an attempt at playfulness.

'Let me give you a piece of advice,' said Mrs Leversage. 'If you can't have the real thing, go without. Cheap imitations are as bad as lies. I'm surprised at you, quite honestly.'

'But it's just a joke,' protested Jane. 'Jim bought it for me when we were in Brighton last weekend. He sang me that hymn about A man that looks on glass, On it may stay his eye. We *pretended* it was a diamond, you see.'

'I fail to understand the pleasure to be gained from pretence,' said Mrs Leversage, increasingly judgmental. She extended one sallow jewel-laden hand to the centre of the table for their mutual examination.

'*That* is the real thing,' she said heavily. The diamond above her wedding ring sparkled busily, full of its own expensive inner lights. Jane stared at it obediently. She felt that the morning had gone wrong, but could not tell how or why.

'Are you sure your friend Jim values you at your true worth? Because you're an unusually beautiful girl, you know. Exquisite. That eggshell complexion with the Titian hair. No need to look so bashful. False modesty is as unattractive as false jewellery. I really must introduce you to my friend in television. He's in charge of casting the new production of *The Haycrofts of Haycroft Hall*.'

'Do you know *television* people?' breathed Jane.

'Of course I do, my dear,' said Mrs Leversage with a glittering laugh. 'You must come along to one of my little parties and I'll make sure you meet the useful ones. But first, you must *promise* me not to wear that monstrosity!' She laughed again, and stood up. 'Shall we take a turn around the garden?'

Jane followed the sulky high-heeled figure across the lawn. She herself lived in the basement flat of the house next door, and access to the garden was not one of the landlord's little generosities. The Leversage's house, of course, had retained its late eighteenth-century integrity, remaining unpartitioned and unsullied by property developer or tenant. Jane considered the garden to be its greatest glory, so clean and full of birds and rich freshness that it was like Eden after her own daily London scene.

'Oh, you are so *lucky*,' she breathed, staring at the drops of taut-skinned rainwater which sat on the glossy leaves. It had rained in the night, and all the plants were still wet and extravagantly green. The lawn glinted like an emerald. Violent sunshine lit the individual delicacies of each grass blade and every leaf in this wealthy frondescence.

Mrs Leversage had instructed her gardener to plant as many separate varieties of flower and shrub as was humanly possible in the space, and the result was a thickly embroidered spectacle, a *mille fleurs* tapestry in the medieval manner, an impossibly detailed treasury of newly minted shrubs, saplings, creepers, bracken and enamelled flowerets.

The two women moved lazily from plant to plant, Mrs Leversage inspecting each one with a beady eye for less than perfect health. Jane traced their outlines with her fingertips and sniffed at them like a blind girl. She had forgotten the sharp conversation and her own unease in a kind of verdurous ecstasy.

'I would never want to go anywhere else if I were you,' she said. 'I think I would be perfectly happy.'

Mrs Leversage paused at a rose bush to snap off a fading crimson head.

'Tell me about your "Jim",' she said. 'What exactly do you see in him? Would I be right in deducing from my own chance observations that he is, if you will excuse the wisecrack, something of a rough diamond?'

'Jim is Jim,' said Jane stupidly. 'I don't know. I don't seem to think like that.'

'It is never too soon to start asking yourself, what do *I* want from this relationship? You must say to yourself *constantly*: Am I getting as much back as I am putting into it?'

'We have quarrels sometimes, if that's what you mean, but I suppose most people do,' said Jane, with a cloudy face. 'I met him at a party. He'd had a bit to drink, and he was singing with his eyes shut. He has a lovely voice. I liked the way he said the words of the song. We moved in together when this flat came up.'

Mrs Leversage raised her eyebrows and stayed silent.

They continued their walk to the end of the garden, where pear trees grew in fruit-clustered ladders up the brick wall. This orchard corner also sheltered green peaches, under-ripe damsons, and an apple tree loaded with early burnished fruit. Mrs Leversage raised her arm and plucked down two apples. She polished them graciously against the sleeve of her silk dress, then offered one to Jane. She watched the girl's teeth broach the fruit's white sparkle.

'Of course, things are different these days,' she said deliberately. 'But I'm not all that much older than you. Maybe ten years. Twelve at most. I would never have agreed to live with a man without at least the offer of marriage. What *is* there to look forward to otherwise? The woman is always the loser in such a relationship. She leaves the man no incentive. As my mother used to say, "Why buy a cow when you can milk it for nothing?"'

Jane felt suddenly tired and close to tears. Her pleasure in the garden had evaporated. She could not remember saying anything in particular, but knew she must have made a bad mistake somewhere along the line. She had unintentionally offended Mrs Leversage, who had been so kind in asking her to lunch on her day off. She glanced at her, noticing the discontented fold of her mouth, and the sinuous restlessness of her hands around the apple.

With a great effort to return to less painful ground, she asked, 'Is it true that *real* diamonds will write on glass?' Mrs Leversage's face cleared. She even smiled. Jane beamed back in relief.

'Yes, my dear. They are the hardest natural substance known to man. How strange that you should ask that! You've reminded me of the first man I nearly married. He was young, he had a brilliant future ahead of him, and he was wild about me. One evening he proposed to me – I remember it was at the Caprice. Do you know it? No. Well. *Anyway.* He gave me the largest solitaire ring you ever saw. I wouldn't say yes or no. The diamond mesmerised me. I hesitated, then accepted. But as the evening wore on, I knew I had made a terrible mistake. To cut a long story short, I made some excuse, slipped away from the table, escaped from the restaurant to where his car was parked a few spaces away, and . . . Can you guess what I did?'

'No,' said Jane earnestly.

'On the windscreen in large letters I used the diamond to scratch the words, "*Sorry. No go.*" And I have never regretted doing that. Because, remember, Jane, it is *so* important to be true to oneself. I cannot emphasise that enough, my dear.'

'What happened to the diamond?' breathed Jane.

'I still have it,' said Mrs Leversage with a misty smile.

They stood in thoughtful silence for some moments.

'That diamond was the perfect medium for my message,' mused Mrs Leversage. 'I have always refused to be forced into compromises. What is it Shakespeare says about integrity? Something to do with a jewel. I'm sure he must have meant a diamond.'

She gave Jane's cheek a pinch, then sauntered back towards the house.

'Let's have some lunch now,' she called back over her shoulder.

Jane stayed another moment, lifting her face to the garden-spiced breeze. She snuffed the air like a cat or a dog. Its rich warmth made her wish foolishly for the brine-freshened gales of her last weekend in Brighton. The sun was at its height, pulling all the moisture in the garden back to itself. The heat and dampness produced giddy scents, and insects hummed greedily. A bee boomed like a threat in her ear. She took to her heels, across the lawn, and into the cool house.

'I hope you don't mind taking pot luck like this,' said Mrs Leversage as they sat in the sepia shade of the dining room over the remains of last night's dinner. Jane's eyes were still dazzled by the garden, and in this interior gloom she could make out little but the sharkish whiteness of Mrs Leversage's smile.

'It's delicious,' she replied in docile gratitude. They were attacking the broken coral ramparts of a salmon mousse.

Mrs Leversage poured the last of a chilly bottle of Sancerre.

'There is something so sad about eating left-overs on your own. Don't you agree?' she apostrophised in her habitual dinner-party manner.

'I never seem to have much left over because of Jim's appetite,' said Jane seriously. 'But I always throw out some bread for the birds.'

'I'm not sure how well Beef Wellington stands repetition,' said Mrs Leversage. 'So I will content myself with a little of this deliciously ripe Brie. But help yourself, my dear, by all means.' She hesitated, then opened a bottle of the bargain claret which her husband refused to drink.

'What number of wedding anniversary was it, Mrs Leversage?' asked Jane, tearing her eyes away from the rosy slices of beef on her plate.

'Our fifth,' said Mrs Leversage, with downcast eyes and a modest smile. Then she looked up dramatically from under her brows, transfixing Jane with a needle-sharp stare.

'We have the perfect marriage,' she said, with considerable simplicity.

Jane gave a tentative smile, rapidly replacing this with what she hoped was a more appropriate expression of awe. She thought of the fat man she had met once or twice in the street, and of the pale brown eyes prominent behind their bifocals. Toad-coloured was how she had described them to Jim. She blushed.

'I hope one day, Jane, that you will find happiness like this with a man,' continued Mrs Leversage. 'I think, if you will forgive me for saying so, that you are not critical or exacting enough. You must put a man on his mettle to find out just what he is worth.'

Jane paused in mid-mouthful and considered this.

'Whenever I have a five-pound note, I slide it into my purse so that the Duke of Wellington's face looks over the flap. Because he has the same look about the eyes as Jim. Is that a good sign?'

Mrs Leversage's face became enigmatic to the point of sphinxdom.

'I don't think you have taken my point,' she said coldly. She cut herself a long sliver of cheese, then pushed it aside. 'Beware egocentricity, Jane,' she said. Her eyes were very green as she stared at the girl. 'You only talk of how *you* feel. You should surely be more aware of how *he* values you.'

Jane looked troubled.

'I don't think he's the type to show his feelings,' she said. 'I think it's something to do with him coming from the North.'

'I can see I shall have to *show* you what I mean,' said Mrs Leversage. 'Wait here.'

Jane watched her stalk from the room, slightly unsteady in her high shoes. She tried to think why she felt so strange. When she pushed her chair back and stood up, the room span gracefully around her shoulders for a moment.

Over by the mantelpiece, the afternoon sun spilled into the air like golden tea. Jane stood in its warmth and blinked at her reflection in the pier-glass. The wine soared in her head and she was impressed by her own beauty. She lifted her hand to touch the flame-coloured hair, watching the fair-skinned heroine in the mirror do the same.

Her eye became distracted by the forest of precious objects between her and the flattering shadow. Pale cards engraved with a wealth of invitational gold were propped against the central clock and its ormolu cherubs, clustering beyond to bronze satyrs and *bonbonnières* milkily enamelled with lovers. A procession of parties, weddings and celebrations shimmered with the confident promise of happinesses which Jane would never see. It was like hearing familiar music from a long way off, and not being able quite to make out the tune. A tear stole pleasurably down her hot cheek. From the kitchen came the whirr of the grinder.

'Thank goodness,' she murmured. 'Coffee.'

The fragrance of the beans combined with the night-faded persistence of cigars. She wished she could take this lovely sophisticated combination back to her own flat, which smelt musty because of the damp, and of meals more prosaic by far than the ones consumed in *this* house.

'No, stay by the looking-glass,' said Mrs Leversage. She set down the tray, then took up the shallow box in front of the coffee pot.

'I hope this will show you what I have been talking about,' she said, advancing towards her, fiddling with the catch of the box. The lid flew open. Jane stared. Mrs Leversage smiled. The gems flashed their dazzling faces into the afternoon.

'My fifth wedding anniversary present from Adrian. Fifteen emeralds, and two hundred and fifty diamonds. See how thoughtfully he chose those variants on the number five. Emeralds for my eyes. Diamonds because they are *my* stone.' She pointed to the variously faceted gems. 'Brilliant cut. Marquise. Pear-shaped. Trilliant. See the straight square lines of the emeralds; except for that exquisite cabochon specimen on the clasp.'

Their brilliance reminded Jane strongly of the wet garden.

'Just like a tree after it's been raining,' she said reverently. 'In fact, trees *are* diamonds, when you come to think of it. Trees turn into coal after a few thousand years, don't they?'

Mrs Leversage shot her a sharp look, taking in her heightened colour and vagueness.

'And then coal turns into diamonds, although it takes a very long time,' Jane rambled on.

'We must see how they look on you,' said Mrs Leversage curtly. 'Face the looking glass. I'll fasten it.'

Jane turned obediently, staggering against the fender. She steadied herself and watched as Mrs Leversage drew the diamond collar around her neck, fumbling under the weight of auburn hair as she tried to snap the clasp shut. The necklace was cold against her collar-bone and she shuddered.

'Keep still,' said Mrs Leversage, 'or you'll make me drop it.'

'Sorry. A goose walked over my grave.' Jane giggled foolishly, then swept her hair up on top of her head in an attempt to help.

'*There*. Stay like that, Jane. Stay quite still.'

They faced the reflection in the mirror. Jane's arms stretched long and white above her head, and her hands were invisible, buried in the hair they held aloft. Her gem-encircled neck looked not her own. She felt embarrassed at showing the soft marigold hair under her arms, and blushed.

It was very quiet in the room. She saw Mrs Leversage's face behind her in the mirror. Mrs Leversage was staring at her in such a hard bright way, with such an astonishingly unpleasant smile on her lips, that Jane blurted out, 'Can't I go now?'

She felt a gliding movement at her side, a warm pressure beneath her armpit. At the same time she saw in the mirror a sallow jewelled hand snake to and squeeze at her breast.

There was a moment of undiluted bafflement before her brain connected the image with the sensation.

'No!' she roared, only it came out as a mewing noise. She wrenched away, catching a glimpse of her own crimson face in the mirror, and, banging her ankles clumsily against the fender, lost her balance and fell headlong. The patterns of the Turkish carpet shot up towards her face and she clutched at the fire screen and irons which were in her immediate downward path. There was a racket of clattering brass and splintering wood as she hit the deck.

Into the silence which followed Mrs Leversage's words fell like solid objects, plangent and metallic.

'You're going to be very sorry if you've damaged that necklace. Very sorry indeed.'

Zoë and the Pedagogues

'MSM!' said Shelagh. 'Mother of God, how many more times!'

The Datsun Colette heaved itself forward just as the lights turned, then died halfway across the yellow box.

'Sorry,' said Zoë, turning hot inside her clothes. There was the usual fanfare of horns. Cars squeezed round them, then roared off like aeroplanes. In the mirror Zoë could see the face of the lorry driver trapped behind her, swearing like a goldfish.

'Handbrake,' said Shelagh. 'Into neutral. Ignition. What a way to earn a living.' She gave a bitter laugh.

As they crept away, Zoë reminded herself to breathe in and out. Relax, she told herself, but this made her forget about the clutch for a moment, and the car went into rabbit spasms. She felt as useless as she had done last night with Roger.

'This is your seventh lesson,' said Shelagh evenly, 'and you're *still* not out of third gear. That's bloody slow going.'

'How many lessons will it take me to learn?' asked Zoë.

'Usually I would say one for every year of your life, but in your case I'd add your grandma on too.'

They reached a good long traffic jam and sat in comparative amity for a while, Shelagh puffing at her fourth cigarette of the hour. She was a fair fat woman with the milky blue eyes of a child.

'You pay ten pounds for a lesson, right?' she said. 'Well, I only get two pound fifty of that. What about the workers, eh?'

Zoë tut-tutted sadly.

'Into first. Clutch up *slowly*. You know that Wisconsin diet I told you about, it's bloody murder I can tell you. A pound of broccoli and two crispbreads is all I've had today.'

They reached the disused sewage works at last, and drove around searching for a cul-de-sac of their own. Wherever she looked, Zoë met the bulbous eyes of other learner drivers.

'The main thing to remember is your PSL and your MSM,' said Shelagh. These mnemonics infused Zoë with an unshakeable belief in her own incompetence. The letters entered her ears and sat inside her head, but she could not link them to her hands and feet at all. Mirror, she thought laboriously. Signal. (Roger, I don't think I want to see that Russian film at the Poly.) Manoeuvre. (So I've asked my sister over for the evening.) No, it would never work; she lacked coordination.

'Ten to two!' bellowed Shelagh, 'Feed the wheel! *Feed* it!'

On the way back Zoë did something clumsy which

caused the driver of a laundry van to jab a stiff-fingered gesture at her before howling off in a spume of exhaust.

'Men,' said Shelagh passionlessly. 'They drive like fucking rockets.'

Back at the flat, Zoë poured herself a couple of inches of Roger's precious yellow vodka and drank them straight off. She sat down with a second glass and her Manual for Driving, which fell open at the section on steering.

If you are turning left, the left hand should be moved to a higher position (but not past twelve o'clock) and the wheel pulled downwards, she read aloud, *while the right hand is slid down the wheel. You can then push up with the right hand while the left hand, in turn, is slid up the wheel. If you are turning right the movements are reversed.*

All that o'clock stuff was bad enough but not quite so bad as driving past parked cars without scraping them. This inability to judge space was like her father, tanked up, moving along the hall passage when she was a little girl, hand out to touch what wasn't there. Here's the beer monster, his cronies called through the letter box, dumping him on the step. Thank goodness Roger didn't drink; although a couple of times in the last month he had rung late on in the evening to say he would be staying on someone's sofa because he was over the limit.

I must be slow at learning, she thought. She was finding her work at the Poly increasingly difficult, even though Roger was one of the tutors. She knew she was not happy but whenever she tried to think why, her mind stalled. It was to do with Roger, even though she could not work out what; perhaps the fact that she was so much younger and stupider than him meant that it would never be all right.

They told me I was bright at school, she thought, and turned back to the section on hill starts. When she heard Roger at the door she slid her glass behind the sofa.

'My God, what a bunch of morons,' he said, frowning, pushing his hair off his forehead, removing his gloves and adjusting the Joán Miró print above the mantelpiece. Zoë hovered around him while he did his whirlwind impersonation. He moved with conscious effectiveness, swift and forceful, drawing the curtains exactly so, squeezing her breast and flicking on the stereo for a calmative blast of Radio 3. In all their five months together she had never said anything which pleased him more than when she had likened him to Baryshnikov.

Roger's tiny bachelor flat was as unlike her mother's house as possible, most notably because it had a place for everything and everything in its place. He always saw if you put a book back in its wrong stripe of air, and he was bound to spot the vodka glass before long. He was on the short side, although you hardly noticed that when he was behind a podium; in lectures and at seminars his eyes were like coals in that lean intellectual dial, and he managed his voice with an actor's expertise.

'Some people are coming over tonight,' he said.

'Oh dear,' said Zoë. 'I need to finish my essay for Mr Proctor.'

'Ben will be here this evening. He'll let you off, particularly if you stop calling him Mr Proctor. But why the hell didn't you finish it today? You're wasting too much time over that bloody car.' He locked the bathroom door behind him as a sign of displeasure.

Zoë wondered when he would find out about her

lunchtime shifts at Casey Jones. A well-preserved forty-two-year-old, Roger found such food as cheeseburgers morally shocking. 'He had already noticed the smell of onions on her hair. But that was the only way she could pay for the driving lessons with Shelagh. She wished she could plan her own time rather than fit round him at the drop of a hat, like this party tonight, but that only made the sort of trouble that didn't get anywhere. She thought of her parents arguing themselves into stalemate time and again, and the waste of energy. Her father went when she was twelve.

Two months ago, on her twenty-first birthday, she had visited her mother in Essex. There was a card with a key: 'A bit battered but it still goes. Cheers. Dad.' In the road outside was an orange Vauxhall Viva.

'It's only because he's got a job in that used-car emporium outside Chigwell,' said her mother as Zoë tried the ignition.

Roger's friends from the Poly started to drift in from about eight, and stayed until the small hours. In fact they were colleagues rather than friends, and the talk was mainly gossip about absent academic acquaintances.

'Ah, the lovely Zoë,' said Mr Proctor when he arrived. 'As nubile as ever.' He cuddled her heavily. 'You don't mind, do you, Roger.'

Most of the time she didn't have to talk, they did more than enough of that themselves. Occasionally one of them presented her with a question as though it were a lollipop.

'So you're learning to drive then,' said a lecturer in economics. 'Has Roger taken you out for any practice?'

'I've sworn I'll never teach another female to drive,'

said Roger quickly. 'It wrecks the relationship every time.'

'Not to mention your vintage E-type Jag,' said the economist.

Mr Proctor tried to pass Zoë a sodden roll-up but she refused.

'What a puritanical lot the youth of today are turning out to be,' he observed savagely. 'It's all bloody Save the Whale now.' He turned on her. 'You think we're just a bunch of old hippies, don't you.'

Zoë drank a lot of wine and thought about what it would be like when she had passed her test. She imagined the abandonment of parties and the balm of a sodium-lit road in the rain.

It grew late. Roger, who had ignored her all evening, now wore her like a medallion, although he still did not look at her, continuing to talk and laugh and frown his famous frown at the others while playing a painful game of cat's cradle with her fingers. Mr Proctor averted his eyes on the way out. The economist gave a sneer. Zoë thought how wizened they all looked.

Once in bed, she observed with relief that he was in a good mood this time, pleased with himself, his voice chiding with blarney rather than the scarcely disguised querulousness which had taken over recently. Even so, she tried too hard and then seized up altogether just as he was attempting one of his more complicated manoeuvres.

'I've told you before about your elbows,' he snapped from the other end of the bed, while she apologised witlessly and asked him to let them try again.

'All right then,' he said ungraciously, and this time it

must have been all right because he loosed a smug groan from on high and fell asleep. Zoë rolled off the bed onto the floor and lay unable to do anything while her skin burned and her mouth shook.

The next time she went for a driving lesson, Shelagh was off sick.

'She passed out at the wheel,' explained the receptionist. 'Lack of food, apparently. You wouldn't think it to look at her, would you. Big as a house. That'll be ten pounds, please.'

The new instructor had a soft Dublin voice that smelt of peppermints.

'M.S.M.,' she said, before he got the chance.

'Oh, you don't want to be doing with all that alphabet nonsense,' he assured her comfortably. 'All you have to remember now is to take a little look in the mirror whenever you think of it. That way you'll know what's going on, see.'

Zoë started the car and they set off down the road.

'You're doing fine,' said the man, crunching a glacier mint. He started to hum tunelessly to himself.

Zoë's spine unfurled. Her breathing softened and her jaw lost its rigidity. She changed up into fourth gear without any trouble.

'You're doing fine,' repeated the man. 'You'll make a driver yet.' Zoë gleamed, and her eyes flicked expertly to the mirror every few seconds. She saw what was behind her and in front of her, and found she was steering perfectly without trying.

'Since I gave up the cigarettes,' said the man as he passed her his bag of mints at the lights, 'my lungs have benefited but my teeth are falling out. That's right, gently up with the clutch and away we go. There's no need to be putting it into neutral every time; no point in making this life harder than it is.'

Every word he spoke enchanted her, and she felt the luxury of trust. Even when they reached the incline where she had so often perched on the edge of tears with Shelagh, she did not mind.

'Let's try a little hill start, then, shall we,' he suggested mildly.

'I'm not very good at this,' she said.

'Sure you are,' he said. 'Foot on the gas, that's right, a little roaring never did any harm. All you have to do now is keep the left foot steady while you press the right one down.'

Zoë did as he said and felt the car buck softly. She held it there at biting point. Triumph percolated through her veins as she released the handbrake and held them together in stasis for another second or two. The engine hummed obediently. Then they glided away.

'There now,' he said. 'You couldn't have done better if you'd been the Queen of Sheba.'

While she was driving them back to the school, she also realised with the same delightful ease that she would move out from Roger's flat that same week, and if he tried to block her with his familiar analysis of their relationship and all its side-dishes of exactly how and where she was mistaken she would not bother to listen, she would not be deflected by the rights and wrongs and stories about nights away on sofas, no, instead she would tell him such words were a waste of breath, and that she was off for the obvious simple reason appearing to her in this well-lit moment, that she did not like him.

Send One Up For Me

The light had gone, but Tess could hear it was pouring again by the hiss of car tyres. She retrieved her rain-spangled packet of sausages from the outside windowsill, then lumbered around the room collecting saucepan, frying pan, knife and fork, and, from inside the wardrobe, a net of sprouts. She was trying to slim, so had not bought potatoes.

Very slowly, like a circus elephant, she struggled down onto her haunches, then pressed her ear to the floor. Through the grubby piece of carpet wafted the noise of 'Light's Abode, Celestial Salem'. Good. Mrs Waley was watching *Songs of Praise*.

Tess put her food and pans into a carrier bag for the stealthy advance downstairs in the dark. Brighter than the heart can fancy, she crooned under her breath to the television's distant keening; mansion of the-er highest king. The ribbed plastic coating which Mrs Waley had chosen to protect her stair carpet from the feet of tenants rasped beneath her shoes.

As always, the kitchen light socket was empty. Mrs Waley carried a bulb round in her apron pocket to illuminate whichever room she was visiting for more than a few minutes. Tess did not dare follow her example, as Mrs Waley had an unpredictable temper, and that was putting it mildly.

She sat munching sprouts by the light of her pocket torch and thought back to three weeks ago when it had all promised so well. Mrs Waley had seemed a nice old lady who was letting rooms in her Balham house for security and to supplement her pension. For forty pounds a week Tess had been promised the use of her washing machine and kitchen whenever they were free.

Now Mrs Waley came into the kitchen, sighing and moaning like the east wind.

'Oh goodness gracious, I didn't mean this house to be a bedsit,' she began, her eyes everywhere in the crepuscular kitchen but on Tess's plate. 'I've done the wrong thing, the house is no longer my own, I didn't mean my last home to be full of strangers.'

'I'll wash up very carefully. You won't even know I was here,' mumbled Tess. 'You did say this was where I could eat.'

Mrs Waley called Tess a liar and told her not to touch the washing machine or she'd have the police round, then returned to her television. Tess sat on in the dark and grizzled over the remaining sprouts. She would have to start looking for another room again. It was under a month since she had last done this and the horrors of stalking the *A-Z*'s least inviting pages in this sort of weather after work were still fresh in her mind.

*

136

Work was mere escapism compared to evenings and weekends, reflected Tess, as she typed her way through Monday morning. 'We are pleased to announce the completion of this superb block of newly converted flats close to all the amenities of Victoria including the Army & Navy stores, etc.' she typed from Caroline's scrawl, progressing to details about extractor fans, spotlights, mixer taps and the occasional delightful patio. Her desk looked out onto a quiet nougat-coloured street slippery with wet sycamore leaves, bristling with scaffolding and estate agents' boards which included those of Ratcliffe & Staunton, her employers.

At the other end of the room, Caroline and Emma were smoking untipped Gauloises with conscious elegance. They inhaled emphatically, narrowed their eyes and, with fish-like pouting, ejected little blue clouds.

'Who *is* she?' said Emma softly, as they watched Tess's bitten hands move over the keys. 'I mean, *where* does she *come* from?' Emma was lean and leathery-faced, a self-styled satirist.

'Oh, Tess is all right. She's just a bit slow,' said Caroline, shifting her leg in its plaster cast (a souvenir from the slopes) to a more comfortable position.

'Just look at her! She's a great pop-eyed lump. She looks like she's from another planet. I doubt she even knows the *meaning* of body pride,' continued Emma.

Caroline admitted that Tess was overweight; all right, then, gross, if Emma wanted to describe her like that.

'And she's so *dim*!' said Emma with unnecessary gaiety. Caroline smiled wanly. She remembered their school days, when Emma, an anorexic and unpopular girl, had first latched on and claimed her as 'friend'. Emma had not been exactly top of the class even then.

'Well, we've all three ended up working in the same room,' she pointed out.

'You know it's different for us,' snapped Emma. 'But that barrel of lard has dead-end written all over her. Hasn't she even *thought* about what will happen to her when we go computerised?'

'Poor old Tess,' murmured Caroline. She stubbed out her cigarette and limped over towards the window. Tess looked up abstractedly.

'When did Mr Ratcliffe say he wanted the details on Moreton Street? I can't get them done by three o'clock after all.'

'Don't worry. He's out on one of his long lunches today,' said Caroline; and then, heaving her plaster cast forward on a kind impulse, 'I wondered if you'd like to add your signature to my leg, Tessie.'

On the way back Tess bought a bottle of sherry from an off-licence in Victoria Street to nerve herself for the bath which she had been delaying for the past week. It would have to be another torchlit affair. In front of her an old man who had obviously not had a bath for several weeks or possibly months was haggling with the sales assistant over the price of a quarter-bottle of Bells.

'I'm afraid we don't operate a barter system, sir,' snapped the assistant as the old man offered his donkey jacket in lieu of the missing eighty pence.

'Oh, for pity's sake!' snapped the woman behind Tess. Undeterred, the old man was continuing the long and pungent business of removing his jacket. Tess thought about a donation to speed things up, but, reminding herself exactly how much was in her purse, thought better of it.

'Close to the amenities of Victoria,' she muttered as she ploughed comfortably through half a sliced loaf with a block of cheese and drank several glasses of the warm brown sherry. 'Including the Army & Navy Stores, etc.' She began the depressing business of undressing. Strange that the dinted extra padding of flesh seemed to make her feel colder rather than well-insulated. In the wardrobe mirror she noticed how the goosepimples on her arms and thighs gave her the appearance of freshly plucked poultry. She looked away fast and concentrated on thinking her own thoughts.

Sponging herself down while holding herself ready to spring to the boltless door should she hear Mrs Waley climbing the stairs, she sang the 'Skye Boat Song' through chattering teeth. Back in her bedroom, the shivering would not stop until she had put on all her jumpers beneath a dressing gown and crawled into the bed's welcome hole. Here she drank more sherry and sang 'Strangers in the Night' softly and with emotion.

There was a drumming at the door, and quick as a flash the bottle was inside the wardrobe.

Mrs Waley tried to push past, but Tess stood blocking her way.

'I'm not having it, the bathroom cannot be used by all and sundry,' said Mrs Waley, who did not believe in greetings or prefaces. 'If you don't make an appointment to use it there will be chaos. I should never have agreed to take girls, with their wet stockings hanging up making the room damp.'

'Tights,' said Tess. 'Is that why you charge me more than the boys on the third floor? I met Simon on the stairs and he told me you only charge him eighteen pounds.'

At this, Mrs Waley went berserk, stamping her little feet and shouting. 'It's a conspiracy!' she raged, 'You've been stirring them all up!'

'No, I haven't,' said Tess reassuringly, buoyed up by the sherry. 'But it *isn't* fair, *is* it.'

Mrs Waley went quiet, and the two red patches on her cheeks grew redder.

'I'm very tired after my day at work, so I'll say goodnight,' said Tess and closed the door.

'Carry the lad that's born to be king,' she warbled, tunnelling her way back into bed. 'Baffled their foe.'

Five minutes later came another tapping. Yemi from across the corridor stood there with a bumper packet of Prawn Cocktail crisps.

'That was a brave feat,' she whispered.

Tess invited her in, and poured the last of the VP.

'Best of British,' she said, handing her the glass.

Yemi sat on the edge of the bed and refused the sherry, explaining that she was a Seventh Day Adventist and so avoided alcohol, cigarettes, tea, coffee and all unnatural stimulants.

'So how do you get by?' asked Tess.

Yemi shrugged and smiled broadly.

'People say, everything's all right in moderation,' she said. 'But moderation is very difficult. Much easier is, All or Nothing.' Tactfully she averted her eyes from the empty bottle.

'It keeps me cheerful,' said Tess.

'My joy is in the Lord,' said Yemi. Tess sighed noisily.

She opened the crisps and they sat side by side on the bed rhythmically working through them.

'I hate this place,' said Tess. 'I wish I could live somewhere where I couldn't be chucked out. I wouldn't care what it was like.'

'I have rented many rooms,' said Yemi, 'and they are all the same to me.'

'Mrs Waley's a Bible basher too,' said Tess.

'Bible basher!' chimed Yemi, and laughed.

'At work they say it's just a matter of getting your foot on the first rung,' said Tess, back on her old track. 'The mortgage people lend you three times what you earn, but even so at that rate I'd have to earn three times more than what I earn now before I could afford even a studio flat round *here*.'

Yemi shook her head and giggled.

'They tell you to *save*,' said Tess. 'I *can't* save on what I earn. It hardly keeps me in sherry.'

'You worry too much,' said Yemi.

'I know,' said Tess. 'Next thing you'll say is, trust in the Lord.'

Yemi was examining the bookshelf. She pulled out a Bible.

'That's Mrs Waley's,' said Tess. 'The only free extra that comes with this room.'

'This is *old*,' frowned Yemi as she leafed through it with expertise. 'She should buy some in normal English so it goes to your heart straight away.'

'Okay,' said Tess resignedly. 'You're not going to let me get away without the Good News. I've heard it before, but that won't stop you.'

'Too right,' said Yemi. 'Let's hear it from Matthew.'

She sat up straight and formalised her face so that her mouth was stern and her cast-down eyelids gleamed like the backs of teaspoons.

'Take no thought for your life,' she intoned, 'what ye shall eat, or what ye shall drink; nor yet for your body, what ye shall put on. Is not the life more than meat, and the body than raiment?'

'That makes me so mad,' said Tess. 'Where's it all supposed to come from, then? You've got to *eat*, for God's sake.'

'Behold the fowls of the air,' continued Yemi with measured sonorousness, 'for they sow not, neither do they reap, nor gather into barns; yet your heavenly Father feedeth them.'

'Birds lose half their body weight every day in winter,' said Tess. 'Two days and they've had it.'

'Our flesh shall be transformed,' said Yemi absently. 'Maybe we should sing now.'

'Something holy, of course?'

Yemi wheezed in mock-apology. Tess launched herself into 'Brightest and Best of the Sons of the Morning'. Yemi started to improvise a descant, but had to stop when Tess started sniffing and gulping during the second verse.

'The words are so sad,' she whimpered with a hiccup. 'Cold on His cradle the dew-drops are shining.' Yemi stood up and shook crisp crumbs from her lap.

'I must go,' she said.

'Can I pat your hair?' asked Tess. 'There was a black girl at school used to let me pat her hair; lovely and springy, like moss.'

'Another time,' said Yemi. 'You go to sleep now.'

'Send one up for me,' giggled Tess as the door closed.

That night she dreamed she was standing thigh-deep in a field of lilies, ready to go bird's-nesting. She was wearing a donkey jacket and the sun was beating down. 'Speed bonny boat,' she sang again and again, filling her lungs so that she became buoyant and able to float several steps at a time above the ground, moving faster than witches, faster than foxes.

'Please, please,' she shouted, trying to curl herself up into a particularly inviting crow's nest. But the shaking would not stop. She woke up.

Mrs Waley was standing by her bed, shaking her by the shoulder. Tess groaned and covered her eyes to block the sight of the night-greased face and front hair pinned into snails.

'I'm being terrorised in my own house,' stormed Mrs Waley. 'I don't dare sleep at night for fear of what you might do, you great fat trollop.'

'What?' said Tess, still submerged in her dream.

'Conspiracy,' she hissed. 'I've been suffering from my old gall-stone trouble ever since you moved in.'

Awake now, Tess was seized by a fit of the giggles. She lay shuddering and heaving under the coverlet while Mrs Waley ranted on.

'You may well laugh! And as for that hottentot across the corridor, she's all part and parcel of it. I heard you two last night, plotting. *I* heard you, singing so-called hymns. Well, one thing I *won't* have in my house is blasphemy.'

There was a pause. Tess had stuffed some sheet into her mouth, but tears still spurted from the corners of her eyes.

'Black as the ace of spades,' added Mrs Waley thoughtfully. She wandered over towards the door, then turned and eyed Tess with new spite.

'I want you out by this evening,' she said, suddenly calm. 'My son will come round and if you aren't gone, lock, stock *and* barrel, he'll put your stuff out on the pavement. And there's to be no talk of deposits. Nothing but talk of moneymoneymoney these days. Never give in to bullies, that's my motto. I may be only an old-age pensioner but I didn't live through the doodlebugs for nothing.'

Some while after she had gone, Tess sat up and pulled on her dressing gown. She saw from her clock that it was still before six.

She went to the window and looked out at the empty street. The sun was already strong, straw-coloured, magnanimous towards the dust-bloomed privet hedges and tub-bound daffodils, winking from car wing mirrors and the hundred-year-old stained glass of front door panels. Looking harder, Tess noticed plaster acanthus leaves sprouting above lintels and a glittering snail track on the bonnet of the sporty little Triumph parked opposite. Outside her own window the flowering cherry shook a handful of whiteness into the early wind, and next door's striped cat trotted by with an air of modest purpose, while Tess found to her rage that she was crooning 'Strangers in the Night' quite cheerfully as though nothing much was the matter.

The Seafarer

'Oh, *thank* you, Mr Ericson,' she breathed. 'I've always wanted to travel.'

Back at the flat she tried not to crow over Peter. His job at the bank was safe, yes, but then it would never involve a business jamboree along the coast of Norway. Sally's position as personal assistant to the head of Ericson Public Relations and, to be honest, her own personality, had earned her this assignment.

'I bet old Ericson wanted to get out of going himself,' was all that pen-pushing Peter would say.

The Hurtigruten steamer sailed at midnight. Bergen's lights stretched into stilts on the harbour's ink, streaming from there across hollow lifeboats, portholes and the blondness of coiled rope. Sally felt her face stiffen in the salty air; her hair was already crisp with frost. She leant on the rail and watched the progress of the tug's guiding lamp as they followed it out to sea.

Down in her cabin, she could hear metal coathangers tangling on the rail next door. The wastepaper basket was chained to the wall. She unpacked her clothes into a wardrobe no bigger than a coffin.

'What am I doing here,' she said aloud, but smiling. Soon she was asleep.

At breakfast, her beefy fellow passengers tackled rollmops, prunes and slices of fuschia-pink salami with apparent gladness. It was certainly the cold light of day, she thought, as she watched their dewlaps working. Nobody else in the dining room was under the age of seventy, nor spoke a language understood to Sally, who knew only English.

Soon, parcelled up in sealskin boots and suede helmets, they were stamping and thwacking their padded sides up on the passenger deck. Sally stood at the rail again, trying to decipher the coastline through opaque fog, telling over the several winters she had wasted in Peter's company, listening to the slam of the waves while sudden regret sighed hot as indigestion inside her. She had not packed the right clothes and soon her hands were palely cerulean. Sorrow freshened again when she remembered her father.

At Trondheim, a young man stood waiting to embark, hunched as a cormorant against the wind, dodging from foot to foot. Sally shifted her position to gain a better view. Beneath the cowl-like hood of his oiled jacket she saw angry pale eyes, pleated forehead and a sulky mouth.

'Not bad,' she thought. She had been cast down by the

bleached faces and thin thatches all around.

He had spotted her too; they were deep in conversation by the time the ship juddered out of the harbour.

'So,' said Leif Erik. 'I am an electrical engineer from Oslo. And you?'

'I am in Public Relations,' said Sally proudly. 'I've got to report back about holidays on these ships.'

'And how old are you?' he asked, offering her a cigarette.

'Twenty-two,' she said. 'No thanks, I don't.'

'Ah. I am twenty-seven.'

'Everybody else seems to be at least ninety.'

'Yes,' sneered Leif Erik, 'they are all old krauts, you know. They would be better dead.'

Shocked, Sally stepped back, wondering if he were mad.

'Ah, so you are ignorant,' he said. 'They have come back to see old haunts. Ask your father about it when you go home.'

'Don't be so rude,' she snapped. 'You mean the War.'

He gave a mirthless smirk and a half-bow of sarcastic congratulation.

'You shouldn't harp on about something that was over before you were born,' she said.

He looked around him with such venom that she felt positively placid by comparison. This was refreshing since she was used to Peter treating her like a time bomb.

That evening, Leif Erik sat beside her in the dining room talking at such speed and random that she barely noticed the boiled fish she was swallowing. Lapps have over two hundred different words to describe snow, he said, then elaborated on the temperament of the polar

147

bear which had killed his uncle. The sea was less rough during very cold winters, whereas mild weather built up pressure and caused terrible tempests.

'Let's hope it's really cold then,' she said.

'Once I was seasick to the point of green for nineteen hours on a fishing trip for halibut,' he continued. 'It taught me a lot about myself.' He put down his knife and fork. 'You have been lucky to taste this typical Norwegian meal. It is møolje, which is cod with female eggs and also, in the little jug, a sauce of fish livers with cod semen.'

On the next day it was very cold indeed. The ship trawled in a few fishermen-passengers at Bodø, Svolvaer and Stokmarknes. Hail flew in showers.

'You say your girlfriend never minds when you have a fling with someone else,' said Sally meditatively.

'No. Why should she? And I feel the same to her; good luck, we say to each other. It is a necessary arrangement. Both of us travel.'

'I'd scratch Peter's eyes out,' said Sally.

'But why? Don't you like him? You want him to be happy?'

'Well, yes,' said Sally, baffled. 'I suppose so.'

Leif Erik lit another cigarette and drew on it hungrily, as though the tobacco were nourishing him. I bet Peter wouldn't think twice if he got the chance, thought Sally nastily; I bet he wouldn't wrestle with *his* conscience. Perhaps if I gave myself something to feel guilty about, she thought, perhaps then I'd be nicer to him.

That evening the ship stopped for an hour at Tromsø.

Leif Erik and Sally bounded down the gangplank like tigers. The air was savage with frost. They walked fast until they came to a jagged tent-shaped building crenellated along its spine with snow.

'This is the famous Ice Sea Cathedral,' said Leif Erik. To Sally it looked anything but ecclesiastical; in fact, it made her think rather of the Hall of the Mountain King and of how her father had made Peer Gynt blast out in times of crisis. She looked sideways at Leif Erik. His face was half-hidden by the hood, but she caught a gelid glitter from his eyes. He stopped to light a cigarette, shielding his face from the wind as though wounded, then turned to her.

'I think it will be tonight,' he said.

'What will?' she said, eyes narrowing.

He tied her scarf more closely round her neck. His fingers were as cold as death.

'The Aurora Borealis,' he said. 'You know, the Northern Lights.'

Back on board, they stood watching the sky in silence. The other passengers had all gone to bed. Sally felt her face, and it was like frozen glass.

'It's very dark,' she said. 'I thought you had the midnight sun.'

'Only in summer,' he replied. 'Now let us wait quietly.'

She could not stop shivering, even when he put his arm round her. They stared into the raven's-wing blackness. As they watched, a star turned red, then another winked green. 'It comes now,' said Leif Erik, his eyes bird-bright, intent on the heavens.

Streamers of phosphorescence blazed noiselessly, filling the sky. As they stood sighing, veils of chilly yellow fire flared and soared like curtains in the wind. Winking hard, painfully intense, the stars had assumed the froideur of corpse-candles. This went on for several minutes.

'Ah,' she breathed, 'ah!' and stared unblinking upwards.

Now the eery flambeaux were dying, their long fires blanching, expiring at a funeral pace, until at last the moonless sky showed nothing but a celestial hoar frost. In a few moments even this had faded off into infinity, leaving unparalleled blackness.

Their subsequent congress was somewhat dispiriting. As the gaunt face hung above hers, Sally's mind filled like a sinking ship with images of lost safety, grounded pleasures and the failed warmth of belonging. She felt such a lust for dry land in the thick of it all that she was not surprised to taste bile in her mouth afterwards.

Her hair smelled of cigarette smoke the next morning; she did not feel well. At some moment during the small hours, the ship had passed the Arctic Circle, and the sea was much rougher, flashing green and black with choppy jagged waves like broken glass. Over breakfast they made conversation with an effort. Sally was royally bored, pleased that he was leaving the ship that morning.

'Oh go away, please go,' she thought impatiently when he offered to bring her more coffee. At last he went, and she never saw him again.

The snow-shrouded ship chugged on northwards, towards Russia. Occasionally an ashen sun injected lemon-tinged steam through the clouds, but most of the time sea and sky colluded in muffling all colour and sign of life. One passenger claimed he had seen a whale spouting; it was possible. That night Sally dreamed finny monsters loomed dull-eyed with teeth a-glitter beneath her, their bulk so enormous that she herself provided less than a mouthful of flesh and bones.

By morning, the ship had started to keel and lurch with sickening deliberation. It creaked like a pair of new boots. Sally stayed in her bunk, clutching the sides as her feet rose higher than her head then dipped down again. She felt extremely ill and ineffably bored. They had reached the miserable Barents Sea, and Russia was only miles away. There was a gale blowing, and sea water slapped at the porthole. The stiff little curtains stood out at an angle of forty-five degrees and swung back again. The chair shot over from the porthole to the door. Oranges flew through the air. Throughout the ship could be heard the sound of vomiting and broken glass.

The return journey was interminable. Old people dozed around her like wasted dinosaurs. Their talk was all of nausea; an elderly English-speaking couple at her table translated it for her at mealtimes. The woman described lying on her bunk during the storm, listening to her husband's hairbrush sliding up and down the cabin's linoleum floor. Sally attended with a dead face to the timeless bilingual squabbling.

'For some reason my husband has put nails in the back of his hairbrush,' shrugged the woman.

'My dear, without those nails and also some glue, my hairbrush had fallen apart.'

She marvelled at the impotent stasis into which Travel

had cast her. The minutes crawled by and she could barely move for her great weight of tedious unease. She hauled herself out on deck to see if the ice of the storm could lift her from this stagnant trance. Coldness blirted over her in salt-crests but failed to invigorate. Instead, chill clamps gripped her pulse points so that it grew difficult to breathe. She went down to her cabin and lay on her bunk. The cold had worked some sort of confirmation. She had never felt such indifference, and could no longer imagine the existence of love or disappointment or terror.

This huge indifference meant that she barely registered the journey from Bergen to Heathrow, or even from Heathrow to the flat she shared with Peter. She sat and read his note, then made herself some tea. 'Dear Sally,' it read, 'As you may have guessed I met Somebody Else a while back. When you got sent on that trip it seemed the right moment to make the break. Hope you are well. Lots of luck with the Career. All the best, Peter.'

She noticed that she really could not care less. Idly intrigued, she summoned up her father's shade: nothing. She considered how it was in the nature of things that the first day of the holidays always came, and the last, and how it would be just like that too with other men, and with death as well. Nothing was durable. So what, she shrugged.

She drank her cold tea, considering the voyage with fathomless incuriosity. Only the recollection of that Arctic elf light, weightless, soaring and flaring in the blackness, produced in her face a certain chilly correspondent glare.

Below Rubies

I lay on the bed looking over my shoulder through a tangle of hair, across my dipping breast down to thighs like swan's wings. I felt electric and wanted him to look at me. But he slept within seconds.

I saw myself in the mirror and felt none of the usual shame at my hugeness. I thought, yes, I must be nice for a man, I am big and soft and round with velvety skin. Lucky old Colin. I glowed back at my image, rosy like a goddess in a painting, quite cock-a-hoop.

Why do I cry in the bath, then, when the enamel sides grip my hips and my whale bulk grins through the suds? Back in real life, which does not include such nights as I have just had, my own flesh makes me breathless with distaste. Well, I was born fat and I have stayed fat. And that is the last I shall think about it for now.

I'm as happy as a sandboy under the weight of these blankets. It's very early in the morning, maybe three or three-thirty, and I can't even make out the shape of the wardrobe in the dark.

I don't know I'll bother to go into work. Now that Colin's back I'll cook us both a big breakfast. Though I must return my lucky necklace first, of course, very early, before old Grouse gets in. He won't notice a thing.

Old Grouse won't believe I'm ill, but he can lump it. If I can't take the odd day off on what he pays me for working eight hours a day in that stuffy little shop of his, then it's a poor lookout.

I get off at Green Park, with the lions and the unicorns dancing over shop doorways. Being a good mimic, I slide into subdued respect without any trouble. My voice was never as Peckham as Melanie's anyway. And if you twist one or two of the words you use most often, you reassure them even more; like saying 'vey' as in, 'This is a vey fine emerald brooch, sir.' But on the whole it's best to stay quiet and keep your eyes down. Those old boys have no trouble in talking themselves into buying.

Everything in the shop costs over £500. I never begin to want even the cheapest peridot bracelet, I think of all the jewels as if they were part of the display in a gallery. I admire them, yes, especially the diamond rooster pin with his crest of rubies. But I never think I could have them for myself. I look at them and like them, just as I go to the National Gallery sometimes in the lunch hour and stare at the big Venetian pictures; but I don't feel any itch to own them.

Working so near Trafalgar Square also means it's only five minutes to the Coliseum and ten to Covent Garden. I like Verdi best: Violetta and Tosca and Mimi. It's funny, going to the pictures does nothing for me. I've never enjoyed the theatre either, and all the plays now are

154

about such depressing things too, like multiple sclerosis or analysing marriage.

No, I prefer music and colour and being overwhelmed. Best of all are fairs. It makes sense that I met Colin at a fair.

I'd gone along with Martin, the little window-cleaner and double-glazing salesman from next door. For some reason he was always pestering me to go out with him. Maybe I reminded him of his mother. Melanie tells me that I can't afford to be a physical snob, the size I am; but I'd rather do without than go with little runts like Martin.

I can't remember why I let him tag along; but I gave him the slip after we went for a ride on the Mushroom and on the second time round he had to lean over the edge to be sick. I felt disgusted. He has no courage in him.

Then I walked on my own in the blare, with the black sky whirling over Battersea Park, smacking my lips around a bush of candyfloss, nothing but sweet grit and air in the mouth.

The roundabout flanks of the giant cat and ostrich and the horses with their blood-filled nostrils galloped like swimmers, and I strained to hear the organ tune of 'Lily of Laguna' above amplified Blondie and Madonna. I grew familiar with the faces that came round: the laughing mother with her roaring crimson-faced baby on the ostrich; the Rastafarian as still and beautiful as a centaur; the girl with green lipstick; and the sulky lout lounging the wrong way round on the gaudy rooster, showing off, arms folded behind his head, a leg either side of the golden pole, his feet crossed on the tail feathers, lazing with cocky ease along the back of the painted bird. I kept looking out for him.

From the Wall of Death came screams which escalated and fainted as the machines revolved in the blackness. I started meandering across the grass towards it, and I was invisible and happy.

I stopped at the coconut shy. There he was again, the one who had been riding the rooster. I watched him roll his sleeves up to the elbow. He had a bad-tempered face with the sort of black-fringed eyes which they say have been put in with a sooty finger. Beside him was a small pyramid of the wooden balls, which he heaved with startling violence, one by one at a steady pace, with such precision that a little crowd grew round the stall. He was aiming at one coconut only, and hitting it every time, very hard. It did not budge. The crowd murmured. He threw the last ball with such a vicious twist that it split into several parts when it reached its target. The coconut, however, remained steady as a rock. People began to shout, 'Cheat!' and 'It's nailed down!' The owner of the coconut shy looked every bit as dark and bad-tempered as my man, but not by any means as heavily built. He gave a cross grin and said, 'Here y'are, mate, better luck next time,' pitching over a coconut from a secret store behind the canvas flap.

My man tossed it aside, then hopped lazily across the rope, past the stall's owner, and lobbed the rest of the coconuts to the laughing crowd. I fielded one neatly, and he winked at me with his sooty eye. The stallholder looked like thunder but didn't dare touch him.

'Mind if I join you?' he asked. I swelled with pride. He

latched on. He hardly said anything after that. I was as pleased as Punch.

It was late by now and the stalls were starting to close down. There was that lovely cheap smell of danger. We mounted the Waltzer, the two of us bunched into a snub-nosed cart, and an iron bar fastened us down. Because it was late, I suppose, and because of bye-laws insisting on the right to sleep of Battersea residents, there was none of the usual amplified racket, and they turned the lights off too. It got up speed and we whipped around at a neck-cracking pace. I lost my nerve, my skirt blew up, I couldn't stop laughing, and *round* we went, the whole machine creaking like a ship in a storm; and the screams of those around us on this circular hurtle swelled and faded, swelled and faded. In front of my eyes blinked trees, a helter skelter, the paybooth, his face, in regular crazy succession, and from my mouth belted uncontrollable laughter I could not recognise as my own. Then the unmasked creaking and screams started to sound terrifying; but almost as quickly we were turfed out of the little carts, and I was staggering against him down on the bruised grass again.

I didn't know who he was or where he came from, I didn't even know his name. I'm usually a good deal more cautious than that. I read the papers just like anyone else, I know what can happen. But that last ride had taken away my common sense. I was chuckling at his arm round me, we were giving each other pinches and punches all the way back to my flat, and by the time we came to it, it was as mad as the Waltzer.

When I saw his bristly face on the pillow next morning, I was shocked. He looked like a cartoon villain, with that blue chin and one of those dotted line tattoos round his neck labelled CUT HERE. I hadn't noticed *that* the night before. I turned back the sheet to look at it, the large root resting on his belly.

He growled and woke up.

'No harm in looking,' I said.

And we were off again.

That was the best of it, if I'm honest, of course. I know what Melanie thinks, and she's right, he does sponge off me as much as he can. But I don't care. I love it.

That was only a month ago. He's been staying here on and off. I don't think he has anywhere else just now. I still don't know what he does for a living when he's in work, but, as Melanie said, it's hardly likely to be legal, honest, decent or truthful.

I know it's not too clever to get involved with a waster like this. I know it hasn't been so good lately, either. Take that evil row at the weekend, for example. But my way of coping with life has always been, Ignore It and Keep Hoping. I go from day to day, and I do as little as possible, unlike Melanie. My sister slaved away at school, and was the only girl they ever produced who went on to college. Now she is a trainee solicitor and lives with another trainee solicitor out in Hainault, which was as far away as she could get from Peckham. I went to dinner there a couple of months ago. Everything smelt of air freshener. They talked about grouting for two whole courses, then during pudding about how twenty-seven and three-quarters was the right age to start a family. All the time there was the whine of next door's Black-and-Decker, because Do-It-Yourself is what they do on Saturday nights out in Hainault. Well, I know what *I'd* rather be doing.

I believe in shutting my eyes and waiting for the bad things to go away. It works, too! Yesterday everything looked as bad as it could be, and now we're together again.

That row on Saturday was bad. There was screaming and shouting and hauling each other across furniture. I swung a punch and caught him in the eye. He gave me a fat lip, then he took my rent money and walked out. I spent Sunday trying to get rid of the blue marks with ice cubes, and played the Bessie Smith song about fifty times. 'I'd rather be dead and buried in my grave; mean old grave!' That always cheers me up.

Yesterday morning, the usual deadbeat Monday, I thought old Grouse would make comments, but he was too excited about a new necklace which he'd bought cheaply from some dealer.

'It might even be late seventeenth century,' he muttered, 'the settings are so extraordinarily fine.'

He has a slack throat like a trout and a pair of plain-glass half-moons looped over his lugs in an attempt to appear more scholarly to the customers. He employs me as his shop assistant because I make a good showcase for jewels. I look imposing, even dignified, particularly in the black velvet dresses he makes me wear. Jewels look best of all against black velvet or white skin. The gentlemen can see this, and they trust me, they find me reassuring.

'Try this on for me, will you, my dear?' they say, and I dimple as I slip on the amethyst eardrops or the golden rope of enamelled ivy leaves.

When I saw old Grouse's new necklace yesterday morning, I understood why he was so happy. It was a web of rubies and pendant pearls as big as pear-drops. He made me try it on to see how it would look. We both stared in the mirror and sighed. You know the way, when you try something on and all your friends say, yes, go on, go on, buy it. You blush with pleasure and natural ownership.

Well, it was like that, only better. The necklace gave my skin a nap like expensive writing paper.

That's one good thing about being fat, you usually have a good complexion. I've noticed on the way in on the bus how nice the skins are on the black women. I bet I'd get on well with those women if I could understand what they were on about. They sit there at eight in the morning, plumped down fair and square, acting like they've had three brandies before breakfast, laughing and shouting things down the bus to their friends, and I wish I could join in. Better than the sour old Peckhamites keeping themselves *to* themselves and clutching their shopping bags. Have you noticed how black skin has an extra margin of light, like the silver edge on plums?

Of course, I couldn't buy that necklace. Old Grouse was busy writing out the price tag in miniature calligraphy already: seven thousand pounds. I wished Colin could see me in it, then he would know what I was worth. I looked wonderful as I stared in the mirror, noble and wounded as a diva. His heart would soften.

The idea grew in me all day. I served old fools with diamonds, and for the first time in my life felt resentful that they had money and I had not. I was the same as them, whatever they cared to think; only better, because younger.

Then I decided I would have as much as anybody else for one night.

Old Grouse left me to lock up as he had an appointment with his boyfriend, whom he always refers to as Sybil, as if that fooled me.

'I may not be in until a little later tomorrow morning,' he said; he and Sybil meet once every three or four weeks, and he is *always* late in the next morning.

As soon as the door closed behind him, I packed my perfect necklace in green tissue paper and a proper green box with gold lettering. When it was time to lock up, I washed the coffee cups, set the burglar alarm, and put the green box in my handbag. I went home by bus as usual.

Borrowing it just for a night hasn't done anybody any harm, and it's done me a lot of good.

I came back and sat in the front room with the bag on my lap, and prayed. I concentrated very hard on the thought of him, and I wished and wished until it got dark.

I wasn't a bit surprised when he walked in.

'I'll be packing up, then,' he said. 'Have you got any food in?' He flicked the light on and we blinked at each other.

He had the black eye I'd given him, his eyelashes making a jetty fringe against the jewel-coloured bruises. I did him a plate of oven-ready chips and a couple of eggs. He asked me for a tenner as I knew he would.

While he was eating, I went into the bedroom and changed into my satin dressing gown. I brushed my hair and fastened on the necklace. There was excitement beating in my ears. This was it. This must work.

He barged in, then stood still and stared. His face took on an impersonal glaze of admiring lust that was meat and drink to me. That look will keep me going whatever happens in the future.

We were happy again, like two strangers, and it was as instant as on the first Waltzer night. The next time round lasted more than I ever felt anything, with sleep like a deep snowdrift at the end.

Now I can see the edge of the wardrobe at last. I don't think I'll be able to fall back to sleep. This is an awful time of day, all grey and patient and colourless; it makes me think of death. I used to get up early at home when I couldn't sleep, and go to look at the back garden in my nightdress. It was horrible, the way everything was so cold and even the roses were grey. Depressing enough to make you cry, except you knew that the sun must come up sooner or later and colour would come back to all the corpse shapes.

When I reached out just now, he wasn't there.

Maybe he's in the bathroom. But there's no noise. I would have heard him.

I won't think about this for a few minutes more.

The sheet where he was lying is quite cold.

I'll count to a hundred before I put my hand up to check for the necklace.

How fat my arms are in the half-light, lying at my sides like monsters. How dull and grey they look! The colour of ash.

Escape Clauses

I've just been asking this policeman about it. Now he's reading the paper, embarrassed at the situation. But at least he'll still be breathing at five o'clock and able to go home to his tea.

I asked him about what it would be like and how long it would take. I was stuttering a bit. Well, it could take up to quarter of an hour, he said, but not longer. Can't you do anything to make it easier? I asked.

Instead of taking this to mean I wanted lead weights in my pockets or some such device for a quick clean neck-break, he took it in a sense I had not even thought of. Narrow-eyed at the prurience of the subject, he muttered that I could ask the man to protect my kicking hind-quarters from the crowd's view: for cash in hand he would tie a piece of rope around my thighs so that my skirt would be decently bound in too. At this I drew back disgusted, my eyes overflowed and my breathing started to make a great noise. Also, I have no money.

I used to stay up late watching television, long after Mum had gone to bed. Once I saw a televised hanging. He adjusted the rope around the man's neck, then pushed him off the platform. The man swung and struggled and swung. His legs raced round as though he were riding a bicycle. He burst the cord tying his hands and threw them up in the air once or twice, then started to fiddle with his collar. The hangman leant out and boxed his head whenever he came near. It went on and on, the superimposed digital seconds flickering away in the lower right hand corner of the screen just as they do for athletic events, until eight minutes had passed, then nine. He sent his assistant down to dangle from the man's ankles. This extra weight did it at last. All the time, the TV commentator was talking very seriously about what a terrible man this was, even the shape of his skull showed it (here a phrenologist butted in with confirmation), and how public opinion had been overwhelming.

What bothers me most about all this in one way is that I cannot think what I have done wrong. I've never wanted the limelight. Quite the opposite.

'You must learn to get along with other children,' said my mother.

'Why?' I asked. 'Why can't I just ignore them?'

All that time ago at Primary School, I remember standing in the cloakrooms with a little knot of them – Michael Brownlow, Sandra Hoskins, Graham Doyle and the Bigelow girl with blue plastic spectacles. I was unselfconscious as you are at five. I wasn't aware of thinking or doing anything in particular – I was simply being, which is fair enough and surely innocent enough too – when I noticed they were all staring at me solemnly, shaking their silly little heads in condemnation.

'What is it?' I bleated. 'What have I done?'

'*You* know,' they said meaningly. 'And we can't talk to you or play with you if you do things like that.'

'Like *what*?' I wailed. But all they would say was, *you* know. I plucked at the sleeve of Graham Doyle, the kindest of the four; he drew away with a sorrowful expression.

'But I don't know what I've *done*!' I cried.

'Oh yes you do,' they said, with certainty. Things looked black as I realised I was missing something that obviously should have been built in.

Mr Pringle is my solicitor. He is a cold fish with unflattering steel-rimmed glasses. He has been very patient with me, explaining the difference between judicious and judicial, and attempting to pluck out my stings of emotion and moral warmth by demonstrating that he is but a neutral instrument working within a larger neutral instrument. The law is as finely balanced, he says (with a keen nose for cliché), as a Swiss watch; make one illogical exception, and you throw the whole mechanism out. This is little comfort to me now, for obvious reasons. I think Mr Pringle sees that, which must be why he continued to visit me after my case was lost. He has helped me while away the time with little legal conundrums, for I cannot help going over the lengthy and complicated trial in my mind several times an hour, trying to see the sense in it.

'I have two sorts of hand-writing, Mr Pringle, one with each hand. I taught myself how in a bid to while away the time during a dull honeymoon in the Balearics. From this, counsel for the prosecution Rory Deerhurst deduced that I am practised in all forms of deceit.'

'In fact the Prosecution did not proceed with that particular charge, Mrs Vernish,' said Mr Pringle. 'No proof of forgery was ever produced. Your personal correspondence was openly conducted by your left hand and your business letters by your right. Confusion arose only when you signed yourself in different names.'

'Since when was fantasy a crime?'

Mr Pringle sighed.

'Confusion arose because, in law, a forgery is perpetrated when the hand of Jacob purports to be the hand of Esau.'

'I have never taken biblical names.'

'In any event, the charge of forgery was dropped. I must confess, your calligraphic versatility struck me as, ah, more dexterous than sinister.'

I tittered through a veil of angry tears.

'"Of all the torcheculs, arsewisps, bumfodders, tail-napkins, bunghole cleansers and wipe-breeches, there is none in the world comparable to the neck of a goose, that is well douned, if you hold her head betwixt your legs; and beleeve me therein upon mine honour, for you will thereby feele in your nockhole a most wonderful pleasure, both in regard of the softness & of the said doune, and of the temperate heat of the goose, which is easily communicated to the bum-gut." The defendant has admitted of her own free will that her favourite book is *Pantagruel*. You have just heard read an entirely typical passage from this book. Members of the jury, I would like you to consider for yourselves the probable moral fibre of a person who can find something to snigger at in such unnatural filth.'

'Objection, my Lord. Defecation is a perfectly natural human function.'

'Objection overruled. You may proceed, Mr Deerhurst.'

'Thank you, my Lord. Members of the jury, I would like you to judge whether or not it is likely that a person who habitually reads such lewd and disgusting stuff for their private gratification might not become a depraved and corrupted being. The question of bestiality does not impinge here, although cruelty to animals is obviously condoned in the most appalling way.'

They found it significant that I called my cat Felony. I argued that I had chosen her name for its euphonious qualities. She used to sink her incisors into the heel of my hand and pause a fraction of a millimetre from breaking the skin, staring at me until her eyes were reduced to sadistic yellow semibreves. She murdered without a qualm. She toyed with her victims, smiling broadly at their squeaks and death throes.

'Why isn't *she* a criminal?' I asked. 'Here I am, so criminal that I must be hanged by the neck until I am dead, and yet *I* have never shown such cruelty.'

'The difference is,' said Mr Pringle, 'that we must assume your cat commits her crimes without mischievous discretion.'

*

They raked through my diaries for examples of anti-social behaviour. No luck! As counsel for the defence Howard Vaillant argued, although these journals were full of the utmost violence and rage, they were the very opposite of a menace to society. Just as venom is drawn from an adder and transformed into an antidote to snakebites, skirled Mr Vaillant, so the dark side of human nature grows positively helpful to the common weal when siphoned off into paper and ink. I unleashed an anodyne simper on the jury, who were scribbling away in spiral-backed notebooks. My recorded ambition to do away with the entire Ironside family was in this manner rendered stingless, and I was once more acquitted, although the jury decided informally that my character had muddy depths.

During the last few weeks I have managed to beg several newspapers from warders and visitors, and among these I found the following two accounts of my trial.

Shameless drunkard Flo Varnish crept out while normal people slept . . . and did her gardening in the nude. Busty Flo, 53, has a disfiguring port-wine stain shaped like Africa all up the right side of her body. 'She's really ugly,' stormed blonde neighbour Sue Jenkins, 37. 'Something should be done about it. We've even seen her kissing women goodnight on the doorstep.' And Flo's husband, 42, a fitter, admitted yesterday that they had divorced because they could not live together any longer. Distraught toy-boy Patrick Bacharach, 28, said, 'She's peculiar.

Her cat means more to her than I do.' Florrie, who has no children, last night denied that her father was an Arab.

During his cross-examination of Mrs Vernish, counsel for the prosecution Rory Deerhurst demanded: 'Where would we be in time of war if everyone were like you?' Mrs Vernish replied that she did not know. Mrs Vernish, who is no relation to Cadogan Vernish who last year received a ten-year sentence for his part in the Vernish-Barnes 'knicker-sniffing' scandal, requested a glass of water and appeared visibly moved. She was wearing a dark green dress patterned with white daisies. Mrs Vernish faces seventeen separate charges, the most serious of which is Petit Treason and carries the death penalty. The trial continues.

Waking on this plastic foam-filled mattress, I unpeel myself, damp as a rasher of bacon, and sit up in the dark. There is no window in my cell, but I know it is morning by the clarity in my mind and the lack of soreness behind my eyeballs. Back at home, I'm always awake before six. This whole summer has been wasted by the law. I cannot think of anything which has given me more pleasure in life than waking cool and early in the friendly blue shadow of cotton sheets, feeling life return to its efficient stations all over my body. Then going naked downstairs and out through the unlocked back door into the garden. My toes play arpeggios in the wet grass. Sometimes I sit down in the dew to bask in the silver-fountain glitter of five in the morning. The treetops are lit up like glass, and the air is rank-scented, cold and bonfiery. Against the back wall grow tobacco plants, chives, pendulous tails of Love-Lies-Bleeding, Mile-a-Minute, jowly snapdragons, and the taut caviar beading of blackberries. I go round shaking the roses over my neck; their close-packed weatherbeaten petals store a peck of dew. I stand against the white-washed side wall for a moment trying to straighten my spine against it, and shudder as its still-nocturnal chill lowers the temperature of my torso. Is it irresponsible to court such floods of profitless pleasure? More people should try it, I used to think (before all this happened).

If the Jenkinses and the Ironsides wanted to set their alarms early and climb to their topmost bedrooms to catch a sight of me over the trees, that was their business. I looked up once and caught a row of eyes which goggled at me like fish and then disappeared. Fancy spoiling their children's sleep too. By the time the policeman called, I was always long up and dressed. I would give him coffee and rock cakes while he tried to explain that a public place is one where the public go, no matter whether they have a right to or not. That includes their eyes. Even though my little garden has a high wall and shady apple trees, the neighbours can still see me from their attic windows. So the charge of indecent exposure was added to my list, and Mr Pringle advised me to plead guilty.

Mrs Ironside was never a small woman, and when she stood in my doorway that Monday she looked like a well-built tiger. Arms akimbo, snarling and filling my kitchen with foul language, she blotted out the April sunshine and I resented her hotly. Throughout the wrangle, a cigarette hung damply from her lower lip, and I felt furious because I had just washed my hair for the first time in three weeks. It wasn't by any means the first time that she'd stood there bellowing her wild accusations of witchcraft, larceny, adultery and God knows what. Most people would have gone a lot further than I did under the circumstances.

She left me with a few choice bruises too, I can tell you, being roughly double my weight. But I'm quicker. Whether or not it merely aggravated a dormant kidney condition just waiting for a knock to set it ticking will never be known. Certainly the doctor failed to gain the jury's confidence with his 'On the one hands' and his 'Medical men are in general agreements'. Mr Pringle says it was a trumped-up charge, worse because so serious; it counts as murder, you see, if somebody dies within a year and a day of your hurting them. And of course she had to go and die at the end of March the following year. Heaps of people die in February and March; it's the time of year for it. Even if it *was* her kidneys, Mr Pringle said, it would be impossible to prove malice aforethought and in fact I was acting in self-defence even if I *did* strike the first blow. She should never have said I did that to my baby, rest its soul.

'Desmond Blackacre was found guilty of rape and sentenced to three months in prison. The lightness of his sentence was owing to mitigating – some would say extenuating – circumstances. You were naked and unwary in a lonely public place. Even supposing this to be Arcadian innocence rather than decadence on your part, Blackacre's impulse was understandable and, some might say, excusable. In common parlance, you might have been perceived to be "asking for it". How do *you* view the affair, Mrs Vernish?'

'I think you are talking nonsense, Mr Deerhurst. For a start, I am heavily built, middle-aged, with a twisted spine and a port-wine stain swathing my left shoulder and breast. Had I been a perfect lissome seventeen, however, I would still defend my right to bathe in the River Severn on a hot August afternoon with no one in sight. The fact that Desmond Blackacre had been furtively tracking me some seven miles through fields of haycocks and bullocks indicates that the rape was more than a mere merry impulse. Had I been the one to notice *him* in a Worcester teashop, had I tracked him all that way and managed to surprise *him* sleeping scantily clad in the sun on the riverbank, had I managed to tie him up and so manipulate him that he became a mere tool in my hands, and had I then used him against his will for my own gratification, no court of law would have blamed *his* folly for the attack. Nor would I.'

'So you think he deserved a heavier sentence?'

'That is another question, you realise. As to "deserving", I didn't want him locked up for retribution's sake. If he doesn't know the evil of violation in his own nature then no outside interference will convince him. We are our own self-punishers.'

'A most touching and pretentious oration, Mrs Ver-

172

nish. Doubtless you hope it will sway the jury when they
come to sentence *you*.'

The sight of Patrick in the witness box turned my
stomach. He took a quick look at my face, then his eyes
were swivelling like whelks on a pin. I had to remind
myself to keep my gums covered; my lips were creeping
back in an equine sneer. The other side had produced
him as a character witness, and he did a good assassina-
tion job, damning me with faint praise in all his answers.
Yes, he had known me for more than seven years. He
had met me for the first time in the Sun and Whalebone
over a pint of bitter. We became lovers three and a half
weeks later. He did not know I was married then, or he
would never have dreamed of 'trespassing'. Yes, he knew
I was a drinker. 'I often gave her advice on moderating
her habits, such as, keep a tally on your inside arm in
felt-tip so you know to stop at the fifth glass, and, line
your stomach with a pint of milk before you start, but
she never listened to me. She said she was interested in
Dionysian states of mind.' This of course led Mr Deerhurst rampaging off into the classical undergrowth of his
education, summoning up armies of lecherous satyrs,
women eating their own infants (uncooked), and a
diatribe against the unwomanliness of alcohol-crazed
females, castrating and tearing limb from limb, all of
which baffled, dazzled and horrified the jury. Mr Pringle
whispered to Mr Deerhurst to inform the court that I am
a vegetarian, but this led straight to a charge of drug
abuse. Patrick was sweating freely. I was at some point
allowed a right of reply. I stared at him and powerfully it

173

returned to me, the pang of disappointment I used to feel on waking and regarding his weak profile pointing up from the pillow beside me.

'I accuse you of lack of love,' I said.

'I still can't see the crime in taking a picnic down to Delafosse Meadow.'

'For a start, you were trespassing on private property,' said Mr Pringle. 'Delafosse Meadow was sold by the County Council to Piers Townley as building land a year ago.'

'Delafosse Meadow has been common ground for centuries,' I said. 'I've been eating hard-boiled eggs and sandwiches there for the last thirty years.'

'I'm afraid that is completely irrelevant,' said Mr Pringle. 'You were breaking the law.'

'But why on earth did they make such a fuss about my pepperpot?' I exclaimed.

'It could be seen as an offensive weapon,' said Mr Pringle reluctantly.

I broke into peals of laughter.

'I can't eat tomatoes without pepper,' I wheezed at last. 'Can you?'

'Then there was the knife – ' said Mr Pringle.

'For slicing mortadella,' I interrupted.

'And the stone.'

'Which I found in the rubble where they'd started building. As I explained to the jury, it contained an ammonite.'

'It was a very large stone.'

'Now it's my turn to talk of irrelevance.'

'You did however carry this stone with you up into an old beech tree in Delafosse Meadow.'

'True. I always eat my picnic there; it has a lovely broad branch on which I spread a little gingham cloth and set my food out, so managing to avoid all the ants. It's not very high up, you know.'

'High enough to drop a large stone from. You nearly killed Mr Townley, you know.'

'It was an accident,' I said. 'I had no idea he was walking underneath, then his voice boomed out so suddenly that I almost fell out of the tree and I must have knocked the stone off then. Anyway, it missed him.'

'Actus non facit reum nisi mens sit rea,' quoted Mr Pringle a shade pedantically. 'That is, you are not criminally liable for your conduct unless the prescribed state of mind was also present.'

'Exactly,' I said. 'It was an accident.'

'Unfortunately,' said Mr Pringle, 'you failed to convince the jury of that.'

'It was an accident,' I said, but this time I screamed it, just as I had done in court.

The terrors were with me earlier yesterday morning but had finished by midday, so I was relatively empty and serene for my interview with the new young Minister for Transition. This was just as well, since he had come straight from his weekly visit to the city hospice and was clearly unsettled.

'Some of those advanced cancer cases . . .' he muttered, accepting a mug of prison tea.

'Sugar?' I asked.

'I think I will, just this once,' he said. 'You know, it makes you feel quite grateful for your health.'

'I suppose so, though I can't help thinking it's a bit of a waste in my case, considering what's in store tomorrow.'

'Oh, I'm sorry, I was forgetting,' he said, and blushed like a peony. He was a short muscular young man with an open-book face.

'It does seem a waste though, doesn't it. Just think how useful it would be if they were able to catch my living daylights in a test tube and transplant them into one of your hospice patients.'

'Give them time, Mrs Vernish, give them time,' said the Minister. 'These medical bods come up with the most amazing things. That's an interesting idea actually.'

'What happens when you die?' I asked abruptly.

He riffled through his Transition manual, licking his fingers and looking worried.

'Deathdeathdeath,' he muttered. 'I know it's here *some*where.'

'Oh, don't bother,' I said. 'Tell me, would I be right in thinking you're new to this job?'

'As a matter of fact I am,' he said. 'Does it show? I put in to be Minister for Sport, but when you're making your way in government circles you have to take what you're given.'

'What's your sport, then?'

'I'm a bit of an all-rounder, really. A spot of rugger. Quite a bit of football. But in summer it's back to my first love, cricket.'

I saw a field of happy energetic fools, I felt and smelt

the grassy air and the pleasure of fresh sweat evaporating before it could corrupt. My book was open beside me, and from inside the ramshackle pavilion shone the pallor of tablecloths.

I was so upset that the Minister for Transition took me in a hug and rocked me inexpertly, pressing his mouth now and then to my forehead, until I couldn't see the green picture any more.

We shook hands then, a little embarrassed.

'All the best,' he said. 'I mean, no hard feelings.'

'Not towards you, anyway,' I said. 'Goodbye.'

The Minister for Justice brought his own camp stool to my cell. A pot of Sumatran coffee was produced by one of the warders.

'Do you admit the justice of your sentence?' he asked, almost casually, as he took a sip of the steaming Mandheling.

'No. I can't see what I've done wrong, and anyway I don't think anything would give you the right to take away my life.'

The Minister sighed and took a tin of chocolate Bath Olivers from his briefcase. He did not offer me one.

'It would be nice if, at the end of our interview, you were to sign a statement admitting the justice of your sentence,' he said. 'The government would like it. The people would like it. The press would like it.'

'What does that matter to me?' I asked, not without bitterness.

'Our judicial system is one of the most sophisticated and civilised that the world has ever seen,' said the

Minister. 'A full copy of the Law is given to every child when he or she reaches the age of criminal responsibility.'

'I know,' I said, 'I lost mine during a game of hide-and-seek at my tenth birthday party. So you see, I never really had a chance to bone up on the straight and narrow.'

'A second copy was issued to you two months later,' he said.

I sat up then, and started to go red. 'Your boys *have* done their research.' I said. 'Yes, I still own that copy, but I never managed to wade through it. It was too boring. Any offence I have committed was unintentional, since I was ignorant of the law.'

'Ignorance of the law is no excuse, particularly since you have possessed a copy of it for the last forty-one years,' he said. 'In fact, in law, it figures as the most serious example of contempt of court, as you are now no doubt fully aware. It was absolutely no excuse to say that your ignorance was not contumacious. You were guilty of the grossest negligence in this matter.'

'I still don't know how I'm meant to have broken the law, but I wouldn't have respected it anyway since it is barbarous enough to approve the death sentence.'

'Barbarous? Nonsense!' said the Minister. For the first time he looked a little annoyed. 'The law is a democratic instrument, and the public demands retribution. We do not insult you with talk of the value of deterrence. The law pays you the compliment of assuming that you would rather take your punishment like a man than be lobotomised, forcibly preached at, or subjected to other methods of reform.'

'Why are you going to kill me?' I cried. 'I wasn't found guilty of hurting anybody.'

'Evidence about actual harm done was, as you say, too insubstantial to convict you,' he said stiffly. 'But, as any sophisticated society recognises, retribution is proportionate to moral guilt, not to harm done. And there was no doubt about your *moral* guilt. Give me one reason why you are worth saving.'

I could not think of anything to say. It had been just the same in court when Mr Prosecuting Deerhurst had demanded a catalogue of my virtues. What *could* I say? That I have a way with animals, that I know how to make firelighters? Then, as now, I remained silent.

'You received an education at the State's hands costing £13,000,' continued the Minister. 'Fourteen years ago you had an operation to remove your appendix which cost £4,000, also at the State's expense. You are self-supporting but earn so little that you pay no taxes. You have contributed nothing to the economy, nor have you increased the population. You take no interest in politics. There are no grounds for appeal. You are useless.'

'Live and let live,' I said.

'You can't sit on the fence forever.'

'Who says?'

'We do,' he snapped, packing away his biscuit tin and folding up his camp stool.

I'm tearing round the room now, thundering into the walls. I like to hear the crack as my head hits brick. It's reassuring. The policeman looks worried. He runs after me. He hits my face. I scream. He hits my face again. I stop.

'That won't help things,' says the policeman, panting like a walrus. 'You've got to stay calm.' He takes out his handkerchief and wipes my face with it. My tears trickle down.

The men have come to fetch me. They stand in the doorway. I look in the mirror again and see my life jumping out of my eyes, which are twice their normal size. One side of my forehead is red; I can see the little lines of the abrasion like the weftage in coarse linen.

I troop along with the men. They take me outside. There is a funny little cart with a coffin on it, and they lift me into this. I crouch in the shallow wooden box. Two men pull the cart along. They are wearing black caps and badges and jeans. I clutch the sides of the coffin to keep my balance, and stare at my freckled hands. When I was five or six my mother took me shopping for shoes, and in the window was a framed piece of skin from a man hanged for murder, which had been tanned to show the skill of the shoe-shop's proprietor, and beside it a photograph of the man after he had been hanged. His face was purple; his right eye was open and the left partially so. I asked my mother what happened to the body afterwards.

'Don't be morbid,' she said.

I had no idea what this meant.

Here we are. They help me down. Rearing up against the sky like a bad joke is the angular tree, from whose single branch dangles the ultimate loop-hole of the law. 'People are quite kind on the whole, deep down,' Mum used to say. The man in the black hood has been waiting ever since that morning she told me off for being morbid.

They take me up towards the steps. There is a squeezing fluttering noise in my ears, a battering of wooden wings. I totter along.

There has been a horrible mistake, I want to explain, this is an outrage against the whole scheme of things; but my tongue swells like a mouse in my mouth, and various pulses all over my body beat their drums. I try to speak using my eyes. They swim. I look down, clutching at the arm of this kind black-hooded man.

He thinks I am giving him some money. But I haven't got any. Someone whispers in my ear to let him have my watch. I hold out my wrist and he unbuckles the Timex, pockets it, then nods his head to me to stand by the edge.

He pulls a white cotton bag over my head. It lets the light in, and my eyelashes brush against it noisily when I blink. They are fiddling around outside me. Any second now they will turn me off.

Now my legs disappear from under me. There are distant screams and the crack of gun shots. I am a sack of sawdust, a dead dolly. Somebody has heaved me over their shoulder.

'You're safe!' they say to me, grinning their heads off. There are three of them, large, delighted men with generosity and excitement written all over their faces. The cotton bag dangles from a string around my neck. We're driving at eighty or ninety in a stolen police car, through a blurred landscape of cabbage fields and factories.

'We're the LFLS,' they explain. 'You know, anti capital punishment.'

'This is very good of you,' I say courteously at last, sounding like a Victorian novel.

Extravagant and startling hilarity flies around between them. I can see they are on the dizziest, wildest, most exhilarating exploit any of them has managed so far, even in the extremest extremis of adolescence. Their gallantry is the tenderest and deepest I have ever received from men. I am a queen, a goddess, and my new role is to look warmly at them from on high in gratitude. I stay quiet, but inside my thoughts are of the wet-blanket variety. I suppose they realise they will be hanged along with me when we're caught? We drive on in a dream of speed, and I am reminded of something.

The boys at Primary School used to divide into two tribes, stalking and ambushing and wrestling each other at play-time for possession of the empty milk crates under the horse-chestnut tree. One day Graham Doyle offered to let me be his tribe's figurehead; two boys would carry me round in a fireman's lift, and I would bring luck like a mascot. I refused because it sounded too boring. I would rather have been one of the kicking, fighting biting ones than a mascot, but not even that very much.

This is not an adventure for me as it is for these laughing cavaliers. I take no pleasure whatsoever in derring-do. I am coldly horrified by my prevented hanging, and by the thought that it may only have been delayed. These men, on the other hand, are warm and hectic, boiling over with laughter as we ricochet our way around the anonymous fields. They will probably say fair dinkum when we're caught.

I would like them to let me out of this car without any fuss. I would make a dash for that wood over there. I'd go like the wind, leaping ditches and vaulting stiles, never needing to stop for breath, legs elastic as the air. I'd strip and rub earth into my skin and leave people entirely behind me. There would be a safe hole in a dead oak trunk or a secret place in a thorn thicket. Surviving on very little is my forte – beech nuts, nettle soup, fieldmice, things like that.

But no. I now find myself caught up in some damnfool adventure. I am nauseated. I feel no challenge whatsoever, not even the obscurest hint of satisfaction. It's a thousand to one we'll be recaptured. How long do they think we can drive a stolen police car? There will be road-blocks at the very next town we reach.

Even so, although we are to die, this has less meaning for me than for my brave rescuers, since I neither understand nor accept the logic of such dealings. I am no longer the centre of this narrative, but have become its totem instead; I am the inspiration for these men but not in myself of the slightest importance. *They* are the heroes – if you want heroes, if *you* can make sense of this set-up. Not me. So I must just sit here with my arms folded and let them get on with the story.

DATE DUE